This book is dedicated to Mary, who helped me so much with this story. We are all safer too, I suspect, because of you.

THE FEEL GOOD FACTOR

LAUREN BLAKELY

Copyright © 2019 by Lauren Blakely
LaurenBlakely.com
Cover Design by © Helen Williams, photo by Wong Sim
First Edition Book

All rights reserved. Without limiting the rights under copyright reserved above, no part of this publication may be reproduced, stored in or introduced into a retrieval system, or transmitted, in any form, or by any means (electronic, mechanical, photocopying, recording, or otherwise) without the prior written permission of both the copyright owner and the above publisher of this book.

This is a work of fiction. Names, characters, places, brands, media, and incidents are either the product of the author's imagination or are used fictitiously. The author acknowledges the trademarked status and trademark owners of various products referenced in this work of fiction, which have been used without permission. The publication/use of these trademarks is not authorized, associated with, or sponsored by the trademark owners. This ebook is licensed for your personal use only. This ebook may not be re-sold or given away to other people. If you would like to share this book with another person, please purchase an additional copy for each person you share it with. If you are reading this book and did not purchase it, or it was not purchased for your use only, then you should return it and purchase your own copy. Thank you for respecting the author's work.

ALSO BY LAUREN BLAKELY

Big Rock Series

Big Rock
Mister O
Well Hung
Full Package
Joy Ride
Hard Wood

One Love Series dual-POV Standalones

The Sexy One
The Only One
The Hot One

Sports Romance

Most Valuable Playboy
Most Likely to Score

Standalones

The Knocked Up Plan
Stud Finder
The V Card

Wanderlust

Come As You Are

Part-Time Lover

The Real Deal

Unbreak My Heart

Far Too Tempting

21 Stolen Kisses

Playing With Her Heart

Out of Bounds

Unzipped

Birthday Suit

Best Laid Plans

The Feel Good Factor

The Dating Proposal

Satisfaction Guaranteed

Never Have I Ever

Instant Gratification

The Heartbreakers Series

Once Upon a Real Good Time
Once Upon a Sure Thing
Once Upon a Wild Fling

The Caught Up in Love Series

Caught Up In Us
Pretending He's Mine

Trophy Husband

Stars In Their Eyes Duet
My Charming Rival
My Sexy Rival

The No Regrets Series
The Thrill of It
The Start of Us
Every Second With You

The Seductive Nights Series
First Night (Julia and Clay, prequel novella)
Night After Night (Julia and Clay, book one)
After This Night (Julia and Clay, book two)
One More Night (Julia and Clay, book three)
A Wildly Seductive Night (Julia and Clay novella, book 3.5)

The Joy Delivered Duet
Nights With Him (A standalone novel about Michelle and Jack)
Forbidden Nights (A standalone novel about Nate and Casey)

The Sinful Nights Series
Sweet Sinful Nights
Sinful Desire
Sinful Longing

Sinful Love

The Fighting Fire Series

Burn For Me (Smith and Jamie)

Melt for Him (Megan and Becker)

Consumed By You (Travis and Cara)

The Jewel Series

A two-book sexy contemporary romance series

The Sapphire Affair

The Sapphire Heist

ABOUT THE FEEL GOOD FACTOR

That inked bad boy who's been striking sparks with me since he rode into town? Turns out he's my new housemate, which adds up to a super-complicated living situation and chemistry so hot it should be illegal.

I have a fantastic family, great best friends, a job I love…and now I'm up for a promotion to police sergeant. I need total focus—not a flirty, dirty, irresistible, tattooed hottie riding into my town on his motorcycle. Can I arrest him for being too good-looking? When he kisses me senseless in the back of a waffle truck, it's criminal, the things he makes me think about hot syrup and melted butter. One order of hot, fluffy hookup to go, please.

But the next time I see him, it's not for our date with

benefits. He's the guy who just rented the room above my garage.

I need the rent to pay my bills, not a man like Derek, who I soon discover to be strong, caring, generous, good with kids, and kind to puppies... If I'm not careful, he'll be moving into my heart as well as my house.

***

A no-strings-attached fling with the fiery redhead who revs my engine? Why, yes, that does sound like a delicious perk of my new job in this new town, thank you very much. I'm coming off a bad relationship, and I have zero interest in anything serious. I've got all the serious I need helping my sister take care of her three little kids while her husband is deployed.

Except, surprise! Perri isn't just my future fling. Turns out she's my sexy, sassy landlord.
  A lease definitely counts as "strings attached," and as much as I'd like to get tangled in her sheets, I can't let myself get tangled up in a relationship.

But as soon as we put the cuffs on our escapades, I learn over late-night conversations in the kitchen, that my landlord is so much more than the sexiest woman I've ever met— she has a quick mind and the biggest heart.

Once I'm in, I'm all in. And to convince her that we should see where this goes, I plan on turning up the heat—and not just in the kitchen.

1
DEREK

There are lies, damn lies, and then there's love at first sight.

That's the kind of storybook bullshit that gets people in trouble. I can find my own way there, thank you very much.

Besides, a detour of that sort is the last thing I need now that I've packed up all my shit and moved to a new town.

I'm not running away, even though it looks like it, thanks to the bike and the lack of stuff I own. I'm running *to*, and my goal when I arrive in town is singular.

Do what I came here to do.

Problem is, sometimes I go too fast.

Like today, as I'm riding down a side street on the way to my sister's house, a little speedier than the limit. But hey, I have places to be, people to see.

What's the big deal if I go five miles over? I'm safe as fuck and always have been.

A siren blares.

"Ah, hell."

I pull over to the curb, turn off the engine, and remove my helmet, ready to pull my "hey, we're all in this together" card with the guy I didn't see running traffic duty.

But there's no guy stopping me.

The officer in blue strolling down the sidewalk is certified 100 percent babe, and I do believe this is the best view I've seen in days. Wait, make that years.

Because holy redheaded lady-cop fantasy.

Even that uniform can't hide those curves, nor can the ruler-straight line between her lips hide their lushness. The cinched ponytail of auburn only makes me want to untie it, get my hands in those locks, then run my lips all over her neck.

"Hey, officer. Was I going too fast?" I ask with a *gee, I couldn't have been speeding* grin.

"What do you think, Lightning McQueen?"

"Maybe a little."

"Yeah, just a little," she says dryly. "How about your license and registration?"

I grab my wallet and hand her my license, then the bike's registration. She runs a quick check, nods since it's all clear, and gives them back to me. "Let me guess. You either didn't realize how fast you were going, or you have someplace *real important* to be?"

I flash her a grin, hoping the crooked kind is her favorite. "I do, and I sure hope you'll forgive me."

She parks her hands on her hips. "You're aiming for full forgiveness?"

"Complete absolution. What'll it take to get there?"

She scoffs, but it has the hint of a laugh in it. "Let's hear your story. Tell me where you're going, Mr. Speedy."

I raise a finger to correct her. "I'm not Mr. Speedy. I'm Mr. Take My Time."

She stares at me. "Yes, *Mr. McBride*," she says, emphasizing my name. "And I'm Ms. I Don't Have Time for Flirty Bikers." Her lips quirk up though, like she's trying to fight off a smile.

"I'll give you the SparkNotes version." I heave a sigh, drag a hand through my hair, then tell her where I'm off to, hoping the story of a man looking out for his sister and her kids will win over her black heart.

She shakes her head like she doesn't quite believe me, but doesn't quite disbelieve me either. She whips off her shades, revealing green eyes with flecks of gold—eyes that study me, that roam over my beard, my inked arms, and maybe, just maybe, all the way down.

Oh yes, keep the eye tour going, because I'm giving you one too, officer.

Exhaling deeply, she glances down the road then back at me. "Listen, it's quiet today. I haven't seen a lot of cars or kids or pedestrians. I'm going to let you off with a warning this time, Mr. Lawbreaker."

I bow my head deferentially. "And I'm going to thank you from the bottom of my law-abiding soul."

She chuckles. "Is it though? Is it a truly law-abiding soul?"

I grin, meeting her gaze again. "Right about now I can't decide if I want to break laws or follow them. Would breaking them mean I could see you again?"

She flubs her lips and waves me off. "If I had a nickel for every time . . ."

Well, that's no surprise. I bet each man she's stopped has flirted with her. I'll need to up my game. "Let me revise that. I can see that the way to your heart is through the law, so allow me to follow the rules."

I kick down the stand and step off the bike. As I walk down the sidewalk, I look back at her, smirking, till I reach a stray paper cup keeping court with an empty Doritos bag. I pick up both, carry them to my bike, and tuck the trash into the side compartment. "I hate litterbugs."

"So do I."

I point to a sign along the sidewalk. "And littering is against the law. But hey, look at me, obeying like a good citizen."

She fights off a laugh. "Thank you for handling trash patrol. Now, you need to go."

I mount the bike and tug on my helmet. "You might be sending me off, but don't think you'll be out of my mind."

"I won't be thinking a thing about you."

"But I'll be thinking of you, officer."

"Do us all a favor and obey the law. Can you do that?"

I wink. "Anything for you."

She points at the pavement. "Hit the road. Before I decide to stop being the nice cop and write you a ticket instead."

"Nice cop," I say with a rasp. "I like the sound of that. Maybe I'll see you around, *nice cop*."

"Hopefully you won't."

"But a man can dream."

And that's exactly what I do that night, because I can't get her out of my mind.

Insta-love? No effing way.

But insta-lust?

Oh, hell yeah.

There's no greater truth than how much I want to see the redheaded officer again.

The only question is whether I'll have to break the law to get her attention.

2

PERRI

His tongue is seriously down her throat.

Well, I'm speculating on the exact location.

But based on the vise-like grip his lips have on hers and the way she seems to wriggle underneath him on the park bench, esophagus might even be a good bet.

The blond guy and the blonder gal have been going at it for close to five minutes.

Granted, that's not necessarily a long time for PDA. But let's be honest—how often does one see *this* level of PDA in the town square?

In my nine years working the streets, this has to be the most make-out-y of make-out sessions I've ever witnessed.

"Are we approaching public indecency levels yet?" Vanessa whispers, nudging me as we pass the gazebo on the way to her work.

"Nah. We'd have to have boobs out or wands on display for me to slap them with indecency."

She snaps her fingers in an aw-shucks gesture. "Dammit. I was hoping I'd get to see you go badass cop."

"You're in the mood for a good old-fashioned public flashing just so I can make an arrest?"

Her brown eyes sparkle. "Oh yes. I can picture it now. A trench coat, a belt, a quick peek at some sculpted body."

"Maybe it's not an arrest you want. Perhaps you're a Peeping Tom."

"For the right Tom . . ."

"You do realize flashers don't have *Magic Mike* bodies?"

"They don't? Darn," she deadpans. "But it's still exciting. The idea of having a flasher. Well, if they looked like The Rock or something."

"Maybe you should write a fairy tale starring your very own Dwayne Johnson–style flasher."

She sighs contentedly as if daydreaming. "The thought is almost as delightful as the idea of watching you haul someone away to the pokey."

Laughing, I pat her shoulder. "I'll be sure to give you a heads-up before I make a lewd behavior or public indecency arrest in our exceedingly civilized town," I say, waving at the classy assortment of establishments right here on Main Street—a wine bar, an artisan ice cream shop, a trendy jewelry boutique, an olive-tasting room, and a bookstore run by our other best friend, Arden. I've patrolled this block countless times, and the most trouble I've seen with my two eyes is too much toking up now and then. But that's hardly a crime anymore in this state.

We reach the edge of the square, stopping at the statue of an old dude riding a horse.

Some fourth graders scurry past me in khaki skirts and polo shirts, their matching school uniforms. "Hi, Officer Keating," they say in unison.

"Hey, Hayden, Becca and Madison. Are you rushing home to do your homework?"

"Of course we are," Becca shouts for the trio.

"Good job."

I return my focus to Vanessa, but my gaze catches on the tangled-up couple again. Going at it still. "Sheesh. It's close to eight minutes now. Don't they need to come up for air?"

"Are you actually timing their PDA?"

"Hell yeah. This is impressive. I'm dying to know how long they can last. We're talking serious stamina display right now."

She laughs, flicking her chestnut hair off her shoulder. "I'll require a full update later. I need to get back to the bowling alley."

"Have fun with your balls."

"You will literally never *not* enjoy saying that."

I stare at the sky as if deep in thought then nod. "You're right. I will never not."

She turns on her heel, her cute polka-dot swing dress swishing as she heads off to the bowling alley. I resume my patrol around the center of Lucky Falls, strolling past the olive-tasting room where a peppy Trudy Lafferty waves and asks if I want to try the new kalamatas. "When I'm off duty, I'll be buying a whole bucket," I tell her, since I have a savory tooth the likes of which can rival any sweet one.

"You know your money's no good here, Perri."

"And you know I don't take payola, even in the delectable form of kalamatas. You're still going to have to pay your parking tickets."

"I paid them! I'm turning over a new leaf. I only park legally now."

"Excellent. Keep it up. And I will stop by later to *buy* the olives."

As I turn the corner, Theresa Jansen pops out of the yarn store, grabs my arm, and whispers, "Got the new pink merino wool for you. Want it now?"

"Shh. Gotta maintain my street cred. I'll grab it tomorrow."

She gasps. "Oops. Sorry. I forgot. It'll be our secret that you're crafty."

I mean, really. I can't be the knitting cop. I'm already the face-painting one, and it's enough of a challenge being one of the few ovary-owning police officers here.

I return to the town square, finding the bench couple still in the thick of it. The blonde in the sundress and her guy in pegged pants are on the cusp of a record—close to thirty minutes.

They're on the cusp of something else too.

A ticket.

His hand rides up her thigh, slipping under the flowered skirt. I don't page Vanessa because I don't actually want this scene to escalate to the next level.

I march over to the lip-locked couple, clearing my throat.

But the *ahem-ing* doesn't work.

They are two octopuses curled around each other, limbs circling every which way. His other hand—the one that's not en route to the NSFW part of her—is threaded through her wavy hair. Her hands are . . . It's like watching a game of Whac-A-Mole. One second, her hand is on his chest. The next second, his abs. Then it's destination crotch.

I clear my throat infinitely louder. So loud I bet Trudy can hear it even over her usual four p.m. demonstration of picholines versus castelvetranos.

For a moment, I wonder what it would be like to *want* to kiss someone for this long, and in public. I furiously sift through my memory banks, trying to recall a kiss like this.

But I find zilch in the file of kisses past.

What would a man who could kiss me for hours even look like?

Out of nowhere, I picture dark scruff, chocolate-brown irises, hair that's nearly black with a wild wave to it. Big hands, toned arms, and ink as far as the eye can see, caressing biceps and triceps and forearms, *oh my*.

Derek McBride.

The man I stopped the other day looked like he could kiss a woman senseless on a park bench.

Like he could kiss me senseless.

I blink away the thought since I have no time for relationships, nor any inclination to look him up. Plus,

I have a job to do. Using my most serious voice, I say, "I'd say 'Get a room,' but what you really should do is tone down the level of tonsil hockey in the middle of the town square. Like, maybe go from the pros back to Triple A."

She startles. He freezes. Miraculously, they detach their mouths from each other.

I expect twin spots of red on her cheeks, embarrassment in his eyes. Instead, all I see are two people tousled, frazzled, and turned the hell on.

Lucky fuckers.

"Oh, hey. Sorry." She smooths her skirt, blinking back the haze in her eyes perhaps. "I guess we got carried away."

"I'd say."

"Sorry about that," he breathes out heavily, shoveling a hand through his hair. "Uh. Wow."

It's like witnessing after-porn. "Just dial it down a notch. Or twelve."

"Yeah, of course," she says, her voice clearing as if she's coming out of her fog. "We were just so into it."

"Trouble is the whole town was about to see how into it you were." I turn my glare on the guy. "Your hand was up her skirt in public. That's on a fast track to lewd behavior."

He cringes, but not as if he's embarrassed. More like he's surprised. He sits up straighter, rubs his palms on his jeans. "Are we going to be arrested?"

Nerves thread through the woman's voice as she jumps in. "Because we were only practicing."

I knit my brow and tilt my head. "Excuse me?"

"Are we getting a ticket for . . . whatever this is?"

"It's called lewd behavior, and no, you're not getting a ticket, because you didn't cross the line. But when you're getting too frisky, and there are schoolkids around, you really should consider your whereabouts."

She sighs gratefully, pressing her palms together. "Thank you. We'll practice in private from now on. We were just trying to win."

"Win what? An award for PDA? A trophy for the public affection most likely to result in public copulation? Because that's not something to aspire to."

She smiles. "We're entering a kissing contest."

Things I've never heard of. "And this was practice?"

"Yes. We're entering in the marathon category. The state record is seven hours. I think we made it to . . ."

I look at my watch. "Thirty-two minutes. Keep up the good work." I stare at them, adding, "*In private.*"

"We will." But she heaves a disappointed sigh then turns to the guy. "That was only thirty minutes. Babe, we need so much more practice."

He drapes an arm around her. "I know, babe. We'll keep trying."

They stand and take off, presumably to suck each other's faces some more. Call it a lucky guess.

* * *

At the end of my shift, I return to the police station and check in with the chief, Jeff Jansen, who puts the *grizzled* in grizzled old dude. He wears gruff like a second coat of paint, but he's a teddy bear underneath. That's what Theresa tells me—his wife runs the yarn shop and regularly knits for the man. She made him a fisherman's sweater for Christmas last year, and he looked adorable when I bumped into them caroling.

"Keating," he barks from the hallway door.

"Yes, sir?"

"Did you know that there's a promotion opening up?"

My ears perk. My mouth waters. "You mean for Slattery's job?" The patrol sergeant left for Sacramento last month. Rumor has it his spot is going to an outsider.

"That's the one. I'd like to see you consider it."

I maintain a straight face. He wants me to consider it? I'd like to *be* considered for it. "I'd love the opportunity, sir."

He nods, the expression on his square, sturdy face barely budging. "Good. You're a go-getter. I appreciate that you take on the traffic-duty shifts. I admire that you did the stint in the K-9 unit recently. You're always willing to tackle whatever needs to be done, and your reports are top notch. Plus, you've done a fine job making the department friendlier, embracing the local community. Keep that up. Like the farmers market stuff you do, and any local fundraisers."

I smile. That's easy as pie. "Absolutely. I've lived here my whole life, and I love everything about Lucky Falls. I've told the local schools I'll put my hand up if they'd like to do a Dunk-a-Cop booth at the summer festival to raise some money."

"Perfect. My wife and I are entering the kissing contest for first responders in Whiskey Hollows. It's held at the Windemere Inn."

I blink. "You're doing that?"

"What makes a cop seem friendlier than seeing him or her kiss someone special? It's perfect for our image. Theresa says a lot of local business owners are entering, but man, would I love to see our precinct win."

"Good luck, then, with the kissing, sir. Judging from what I saw in the town square, the competition is going to be fierce in the marathon category."

He winks. "Good thing Theresa and I have been practicing for years." He shifts gears. "Keep up the good work, Keating."

I thank him and leave the station, a burst of excitement in my step.

This is the first advancement opportunity that's opened up in years. A promotion is everything I've been working toward. It would mean more money, more seniority, more prestige.

It would mean everything, and I intend to maintain a laser focus on getting that job.

3

DEREK

One hour to go, and I'll have nailed my first week of shifts here in a new job, in a new town.

Yay me.

It's been busy as hell, which surprised me, but busy impresses the boss man, and that's what I'm here to do.

Henry Granger strides out from behind the metal desk he calls his office—tucked in the corner of the space EMS shares with the firehouse next door—and parks his big hands on his hips. "Last call of the night, and I'm going to need you to handle it, McBride."

I stand, rising from the couch. "Yes, sir."

My partner, Hunter, stands too. "What are the deets?"

Henry scrubs a hand over his jaw, badly in need of a shave. "It won't be pretty. We've got a mighty serious situation."

"We can handle it," I say, grabbing my paramedic

bag so we can head to the van right away. "Hell, I used to work in the city. It was crazy there on Friday nights."

Granger shakes his head, the look in his dark eyes saying I haven't seen anything yet. "Don't get cocky, McBride."

"Not cocky. Just ready."

"Yeah, yeah, city boy. You think you've seen it all?"

I raise my chin. I know this drill. It's all par for the course for new guys, and I get that I have to go through it. The key is to remain strong. "I did work in San Francisco for ten years. I've seen a ton of shit."

"Like what?"

He really wants me to list the calls I went on? The things we saw in the Tenderloin section would make a monster-movie fan flinch. "Let's see. There was the time we had to take in a homeless guy who hadn't bathed in years and had duct-taped vegetables all over his body. Rotting vegetables. Then there was the time a woman drank too much Tide because she wanted to remove the demon baby from her belly. But she wasn't pregnant."

Yes, this is part of the initiation. Share the horror stories.

A new voice chimes in. "Demon baby. I've heard of those. Did it have hooves for feet and a forked tail?" It's Shaw, one of the firemen. I met him at the gym a few days ago.

"It might have spoken in tongues, too, had it actually existed," I say.

He shudders. "I don't scare easily, but demon babies scare the fuck out of me."

"Question," Hunter chimes in, raising a hand as if he's in school. "What happens when the fuck is scared out of you? Does that mean you can't, I dunno, *fuck* anymore?"

Shaw pumps his hips. "I can always fuck."

Are these guys for real? There's a call to go on, and they're trash-talking.

Granger knows it too, and with two fingers in his mouth, he issues a powerfully shrill whistle. "Children, shut the hell up. We have serious matters to tend to. Got a guy out on Vintage Oaks Road. Says he has a bug in his penis."

I cringe but school my expression. It can't be worse than the vegetable wearer or the Tide swallower. But God, I fucking hate dick calls. "We just need to take him to the ER, right?" I ask, nodding toward the ambulance so we can get the hell out of here.

Shaw shoots me an *are you kidding* look. "Dude, you're a paramedic. Don't you think you should try to fix the problem, stat?"

Yeah, I'm going to need to revise my stance on staying stoic. "That's why doctors get the big bucks. To remove shit like that."

Granger claps my shoulder. "*You* use the forceps to get it out."

I die inside. This is the worst. Give me the unbathed masses needing transport, any day. "Okay," I choke out.

He lifts his chin, studying me. "What? Is this hard for you, city boy?"

I swallow harshly, squaring my shoulders. "We're on it." With my gear in tow, I head to the passenger side of the ambulance, Hunter to the driver side.

"No sirens needed for this call," Hunter says. "It's only a mile away."

Granger calls out as I get into the vehicle, "Don't you guys want to know what kind of bug it is?"

Not really. "Sure."

Granger and Shaw join us in the garage. The boss man's face turns graver than I've ever seen him. Shaw looks at Granger, almost as if he's saying *take it away*.

Granger clears his throat. "It's a . . . *cock*roach."

They both spill into laughter, doubled over, hands on their bellies, faces contorted. Hunter joins in too.

I couldn't be happier to be the butt of a first-week prank. I get out of the van, laughing too. "You fuckers."

Shaw points at me. "You passed, man. You passed the initiation."

As I head home that night on my bike, I ride past the spot where Officer Sexy As Sin stopped me. I've ridden this road every damn day since I've been in town, actually, wishing for her siren.

But one of these days, I'm going to bump into her again, and I'm going to get her number and then some.

Because that insta-lust is strong, and I don't think even a demon baby could scare it the fuck out of me.

4

PERRI

"Let me get this straight—you're saying for a full half hour they were just kissing?"

The question comes from Arden as we gather at the bowling alley on Friday evening. Vanessa's joined us for a quick game while one of her employees mans the check-in.

I grab my neon-pink ball from the return. "Like they were in seventh grade, making out after sixth-period science class behind the shed on the dirt path behind the school."

Vanessa raises one skeptical brow. "That's very specific. Oh, wait. That's where you kissed David Bruno for the first time."

"How could you forget? She called us over to her house and made us listen to the story ten times," Arden chimes in.

I bask in the memory of when I first experienced the glory of French kissing. David and I had been dating for two weeks, which translated into going to Starbucks after school for Frappuccinos. One fine Wednesday after a particularly yummy mocha, we stole behind the shed and he planted his lips on mine, and we didn't stop for the longest time. "And it was the most epic first kiss ever."

Vanessa sticks out her tongue. "Only you would have an epic first kiss. You do realize most first kisses suck?"

I wiggle my eyebrows. "I do, but mine didn't. And I've been a devotee of epic first kisses ever since."

Arden raises a hand like she's in church. "Preach, sister. No other kind allowed."

I take the ball, start at the end of the lane, and let it fly, knocking down five pins. When I turn around, I resume the report. "So today, it was a full-on make-out sesh on the bench in the town square. Which made me think . . . when was the last time you did that? The kind of endless kissing and groping that is only that—endless kissing and groping?"

Arden lowers her blonde head, a guilty-as-charged look strolling across her face. "Last night."

I roll my eyes as I wait for the ball. "You don't count. I know you do that all the time with Gabe." She is ridiculously happy and in love with Gabe Harrison, a local fireman.

"We like making out. What's the big deal?"

"But it always leads to sex, doesn't it?" I grab the ball and send it down the lane again, knocking over two more pins, since my bowling game is incredibly, ridiculously average.

Arden scoffs as she grabs a bright-green ball from the return. "Isn't that sort of the point? We don't have to make out behind sheds anymore, or stop above the waist. We can go . . . wait for it . . . *all the way.*"

Vanessa sighs happily. "Sex is seriously one of the best parts of being an adult." She heads to the ball return. "Or so I'm told. It's been ages since I've done it. The penis still goes into the vagina, right?"

Arden nods, her face serious. "Yes. I can draw you a diagram if it would help. It's basically insert-this-tab-into-this-slot, and you're good to go."

Vanessa taps her temple. "Good to know it all still works the same way it did circa 2017, should the opportunity arise again. But for now, I'll live vicariously through your Kissing Bandits."

"Me too," I say as Vanessa takes her turn. "They were into each other, the kind of *into* that leads to tabs going into slots. But it turns out they were simply practicing for this kissing contest fundraiser in Whiskey Hollows, in the marathon division, they said. My boss is entering the contest too."

"Ooh, the chief of police will be competing," Vanessa quips.

"And he wants our precinct to win. Don't get me wrong—I love how the wine-country towns have banded together since the fires to raise money for those on the front lines, but I can't imagine wanting to make out with somebody for that long. Eventually you'll run out of spit."

"Or interest." Vanessa snags her phone and taps the screen. "But there are other categories. My sister and I were talking about it the other night. You can enter the marathon one, you can do sweetest kiss, or even the most passionate kiss category. And attendees bid on who they think will win each category—that's where the money comes from. If you bid correctly, you win prizes donated by local businesses. But all the money raised goes to first responders." Her eyes light up as she scans her phone. "Ooh, they have a category for the best reenactment of a movie kiss or book kiss. I'll have to mention the book kiss to Ella." Vanessa's sister is the town librarian.

Arden pumps a fist. "Book kisses for the win."

I peer over Vanessa's shoulder at the phone, reading the details. "That's a good reason to make out, come to think of it."

Arden gives me a quizzical stare. "Is there someone you want to enter a kissing contest with? Maybe have a kissing marathon with and give that couple a run for their money?"

I scoff. "Like who?"

"Oh, I don't know. How about that guy Toby you went out with a few weeks ago?" She heads to the end of the lane and sends the ball down the hardwood.

"The hotel clerk? He was nice and all . . ."

"But not enough bad boy in him?" Vanessa teases. My girls know me so well.

I laugh. "Yeah, duh."

After knocking eight pins, Arden squeezes my shoulder and adopts a serious voice and meets Vanessa's gaze. "Vanessa, have you met our friend Perri? She only likes bad boys."

I raise a finger. "Correction. I like the *look* of bad boys. I don't mind if they're actually good underneath the bearded, inked, and smoking hot exterior."

The guy on the bike has the audacity to invade my thoughts. He keeps doing that.

"Talk about specific." Arden laughs. "Sounds like you're describing the hottie you pulled over the other day."

"Oh, gee. Was I? I hadn't realized," I say playfully, since I told them about Mr. Speedy.

"Have you looked him up?" Vanessa asks.

I don't know a thing about Derek McBride, except that he's someone who moved to town to help out his sister, or so he said. "No, I'm not going to look him up," I scoff.

"Why not?"

"Because I'm not going to pick up someone I pulled over. And I'm not interested in getting involved with anyone, since I have a promotion to focus on."

"Fine. But you should still enter the kissing contest," Vanessa says as Arden finishes her frame.

"Who would I enter it with? Whether I do the marathon, the reenactment, or the most passionate, it doesn't matter. Jump the recording back ten seconds—I'm not involved with anyone, and I don't *want* to be involved right now."

Vanessa stares at me. "Please, girl. You don't need to be involved to enter a kissing marathon. Plus, I bet you can find someone who'd lock lips with you for a good cause. In fact, why don't we have a little gentlewoman's bet and see who can raise the most money for charity?"

"In a kissing contest?" I ask. "Arden's totally going to reenact Scarlett and Rhett, right?"

Arden stares down her nose. "There are many fantastic book kisses. *The Great Gatsby. Romeo and Juliet.* The elevator kiss in *Fifty Shades.*"

"It can be whatever, as long as it's a competition and it raises money for a charity," Vanessa adds. "That's what we want—any sort of contest. That's what we can do for this year's birthday gifts."

The three of us decided a few years ago not to give each other birthday gifts. All through grade school, middle school, and high school we did, but now we're adults, and we don't need gifts from each other. Instead, we donate or raise money for some sort of charity. We all have fall birthdays, so it's time to start planning.

Last year, Arden hosted a tea at her bookstore, raising money for underprivileged kids. Vanessa held a bowl-a-thon and donated the proceeds to a pediatric cancer charity. And I did a 10K walk to support don't-text-and-drive efforts. They were our gifts to each other, and to ourselves too.

Vanessa's brown eyes spark with excitement. "I could do a bowling competition for charity."

"But you're naturally good at that," I say.

"And you were naturally good at kissing in high school."

"Hey, don't get on my case just 'cause I liked to make out with boys back then."

"You like to make out with boys all the time," Arden chimes in. "Anyway, I'm spearheading a reading competition among the book clubs at my shop. Most books read equals most money raised for literacy programs."

Having lobbed the ball into my court, she stares at me expectantly, and Vanessa prompts, "And you should enter the kissing contest. It's a slam dunk for you. It supports all the causes near and dear to your heart. Plus, your boss will like it. He said he wants your precinct to win."

I raise a skeptical brow, even though she makes a good point. "I don't want to horn in on his territory. What if he wants to win?"

Vanessa grabs my phone. "Just ask him."

I sigh but grab the phone back and fire off a quick text to Jansen.

Perri: Question for you. You said you wanted our precinct to win the kissing contest. Would it help if you had more entrants?

His response is instantaneous.

Jansen: I didn't want to ask you or anyone to enter, but my answer is the more the freaking merrier.

I show his response to my girls, and they smirk in tandem at me.

"See?" Vanessa says.

"Plus, I dare you to," Arden adds.

"And I dare you to as well," Vanessa seconds.

"You dare me? Are we in high school again?" I ask.

"If we were, you'd put up both hands to volunteer," Vanessa teases, and she's got me there.

It's for a good cause.

And maybe I'd like to be a girl who loves spending her days kissing again without a care in the world.

"Now I'm going to have to find a guy I want to kiss for that long."

Or at least long enough to raise a little dough.

As we finish the game, I keep wondering what it would be like to want to kiss someone for that long.

And I keep coming back to Mr. Trouble.

I have other matters to deal with before I find a man to kiss.

Namely, getting a little more money flowing into my coffers.

When I return home that evening, I call my brother Shaw, catching him up first on the potential good news about the patrol sergeant position.

"That's what I'm talking about. You're the *woman*," he says, in the same tone you'd say *you're the man*.

I turn on the light to the kitchen. "Thank you. I'm excited. I need to nab this. But do you know what else this means?"

"That you'll finally crack down and arrest me for not paying back taxes on my secret after-hours stripping job?"

I laugh as I pour a glass of water. "As if anyone would pay you to strip, secretly or publicly."

"Oh, ye of little faith. I have lines of ladies waving small bills in my direction. That's what happens when you're one of the stars of a very popular firefighters calendar."

"You do realize the money is to get you to stop?"

"Yet all they say is 'Go, go, go.'"

"Like I said, they want you to go away."

"Fine, you win the smackdown," he grumbles. "Anyway, what *does* the potential promotion mean?"

I glance toward the stairwell at the back of my small house and draw a deep, excited breath. "It means—drumroll—I won't have to rent the room above the garage much longer. I won't need the extra money." The possibility is tantalizing. A good renter is gold. A bad one is the worst, and I've had the worst. I don't ever want to share living space again with someone who cooks with onions, bathes in Obsession, and talks dirty all night long.

"That'll be a relief for you, considering your last renter."

I cringe, remembering the deceptively sweet

Cassidy. "But that also means I need your help finding a new tenant until then. I haven't had one for a few months, and I could use the extra income till I know what's going on with the promotion. Can you find someone who won't baby-talk on the phone to his or her significant other every single night?"

"It wasn't just the baby talk, if memory serves."

I do my best to try and forget all the things I overheard Cassidy telling her boyfriend she wanted him to do to her. And, evidently, all the things he did to her over the phone. Though in retrospect, it could have been worse if her boyfriend lived locally instead of dialing in from the other side of the state.

"Exactly. So you'll find me someone I'll hardly ever see, hear, or smell? Someone I barely realize is sharing space with me?"

"Piece of cake."

5

DEREK

After my Saturday-night shift, I head to my sister's home, crashing on her couch as quietly as I can, hoping this temporary living situation doesn't last much longer. I love my sis, and she's the only reason I'm in Lucky Falls. But she has three kids, including an infant, and I cannot handle sleeping on a couch much longer.

My greatest love, besides family, is a fancy-ass mattress, the kind that's smart enough to conform to your body. I slept on one once in a hotel, and it was heavenly.

This couch? It's hell on my back, and my back is kind of important to my job.

I toss and turn, trying to get comfortable, searching for a position that won't radiate pain down my neck. Somehow I find one, then drift into the land of Nod.

But not for long.

At three in the morning, a shriek awakens me. I bolt upright and head for the baby's room.

My sister, Jodie, is right behind me, rubbing her eyes.

"I got it," I tell her as I scoop up little Devon.

My sister yawns canyon-wide. "No, I'll take care of her."

But I give Jodie the heave-ho, shaking my head. "It'll be my pleasure." I know how hard it is for her, with her husband overseas for a year, a first grader, a four-year-old, and an infant. Our parents are gone, and that's why I'm here. We're close, and I want to do what I can for her, especially when she needs it most.

"You've got a crazy day at the farmers market tomorrow. Your bread waits for no one. Get some sleep."

"Are you sure?"

I pat the baby's shoulder. "Please. I'll take care of this perfect little angel."

"I'll find you a place soon, Derek. I promise."

"I know, I know. I've asked around at work too. Got a few leads. Finding a rental in this fancy town is harder than differential calculus."

"Fortunately, you were good at math."

I smile, send Jodie back to bed, and warm up a bottle as Devon grabs my finger. "You're going to be fine, sweet pea. I've got your favorite drink right here."

Devon cries again, but it's softened to a mere whimper. She knows the food is coming. I rub my forehead against hers. "I promise. Would Uncle Derek lie to you?"

She coos at me and grabs my beard with her chubby fingers.

I bring her to the couch, give her the bottle, and pop the new Stephen King book open on my phone as my little niece sucks down her food.

* * *

When I wake at the crack of dawn, I have a wicked crick in my neck.

"Morning," my sister says, cheery as can be as she heads into the kitchen, tucking her brown hair into a neat bun. Molly, her four-year-old, follows behind, hopping like a frog.

"*Ribbit, ribbit*, Uncle Derek," Molly says, jumping her way to the kitchen.

"Morning." I pull the covers back over my head as dark-haired Travis bounds down the stairs and into the room.

"Hey, Derek," says the six-year-old with the gap-toothed grin. "Want to go play basketball?"

"Travis, give him a break," Jodie calls out to her son.

"Later for basketball, okay, buddy?"

"Okay," he says, seeming a little sad we're not playing now, and a little happy we'll do so later.

I hear Jodie start a pot of coffee. She returns to the living room and bends over the couch. "Thanks for helping last night. You're a godsend. By the way, have I ever mentioned that a local cop works the face-painting booth at the market?"

I sit up straight, my thoughts zip-lining to one particular officer of the law. "Why are you telling me this?"

She wiggles an eyebrow. "She's just your type."

I throw off the covers, get in the shower, and head to the market.

6

PERRI

Some girls can never have enough butterflies.

They want them in emerald green, in sapphire blue, in candy pink.

A platoon of three-, four-, and five-year-olds skip and jump around the market with painted butterflies on their faces, courtesy of the local police department booth, where residents can learn about our community initiatives and not be freaked out by cops, thanks to face painting and lemonade.

It's a strategy Jansen implemented, and it seems to be working so far. We have a great relationship with the citizens of this town.

They know our names. We know many of theirs, and I believe that plays a part in keeping crime lower than low.

"What if I drank the rest of this lemonade all by myself?" My colleague Elias Nicholson holds up the pitcher, a glint in his brown eyes. We joined the department around the same time nine years ago and have been moving up the ladder together. He's running the booth with me today, pouring lemonade as I decorate faces.

"Then there'd be nothing for the kids, so get your mitts off it."

"But it looks so delish."

"That's because your wife makes amazing lemonade from scratch for you to give away to *children*."

"She is a wizard in the drink department." He pours himself a cup and downs it.

"You're the worst, Nicholson."

He wipes his paw across his mouth. "She'll bring me more."

"She's seven months pregnant, and she's going to bring you lemonade? Shouldn't you bring her whatever she needs?"

"I brought her chicken wings and caramel popcorn last night. And I rubbed her feet. I'm damn good at the husband gig. To wit—I put the baby in her belly the first month we tried."

"TMI!"

"It's the truth though. We went to our favorite spot for brunch—the Silver Tavern—and then once we were home . . . *Bam.*"

"I don't know how she puts up with you," I say, but I'm smiling.

"It's a miracle to me too."

The par-for-the-course ribbing ceases when a

curly-haired blonde in a tutu wanders over to my tent, surveying the paints. "Can you paint my face?"

"You bet I can. Let me guess. You want a butterfly, a unicorn, or a rainbow?" I suggest with a smile.

She laughs, shaking her head. "No."

I tap my chin, looking skyward. "Maybe a kitty cat? Meow."

She giggles. "No. No. No."

"I see we have a tough customer here. Maybe a doggy?" I bark.

"Guess again."

"A horse?" I offer a neigh.

"Do a cow!"

I launch into my best rendition of a moo.

"Frog!"

"Don't think you can trick me. My animal repertoire goes deep." I show off my fantastic ribbit.

She shakes her head. "No, can you draw a frog on my face, Mrs. Lady Cop?"

I smile. "Of course I can."

I scoot my stool closer, dip a brush into the green face paint, and draw a frog on the girl's face.

When I'm done, I grab a mirror and show her my handiwork. "Does it meet your approval?"

"I love it. I'm going to go show my mom and my uncle Derek."

She takes off running, darting down an aisle teeming with tables full of peaches, pears, and strawberries. I tend to the next group of kids, painting a dragon, Spiderman, and another butterfly until I need to take a quick break.

"I'll be back in ten."

"Damn, you women take long to pee."

I punch Elias in the arm. "I need avocados too. Also, if you finish off all the jugs, I'll have to haul you in and throw away the key."

"Please. I know where the keys are."

I take off to the ladies' room at the edge of the market, spotting my favorite food truck a half block away. I jog over and wave to my friend Staci Winters in the window, serving up a chocolate-covered strawberry waffle treat to a waiting customer. "Stop by later, Perri. I'm here till one," she calls out. "I'll save enough to make your favorite."

I blow the waffle mistress a kiss. We went to college together. She helped me in my required bio class, and I repaid the favor a few years later, helping her navigate the fastest path to procuring a permit for her food truck. "You're a goddess of tomatoes, cucumbers, and parsley."

"And tzatziki! Don't forget the tzatziki."

"How can I forget it, even if I can't pronounce it?" I turn around and head to the bathroom for a pit stop. On my way back, I detour through the veggies. I have about six minutes, so I trot over to the avocados since I need to pick some up for dinner.

I look for the affable guy usually running this stand, but no one's here at the moment. I've just reached for an avocado to see if it's ripe, when I hear a voice, all low and smoky. "Hey, officer. I think you might have been walking too fast through the market."

The hairs on my neck stand on end. That gravelly,

too-sexy-for-words tone delivers a wave of sensation across my skin.

It could only be Mr. Trouble.

With an avocado in hand, I turn around, and my eyes feast. How is it possible for him to be even hotter today? Is this a trick only the handsomest men can employ? The ability to multiply their good looks?

Somehow, maybe a trick of the light, he's exponentially sexier in those shades, his gray T-shirt showing off swirls of ink, and jeans so well-worn they cling caressingly to his legs.

Lucky jeans.

But it's his face, most of all, that draws me in as soon as he flicks off his glasses and I get a full dose of dark, soulful brown eyes full of naughty wishes.

Oh, wait. Maybe those are my naughty wishes reflected back at me.

Because I want him.

Do I ever. I want to climb him, rope my hands through his hair, and haul him in for a wild kiss.

Whoa.

That bout of desire was brought to you today by what-happens-when-lust-slams-into-you-like-a-freight-train.

"Gee, was I speed-walking?" I toss out, mainly to keep him standing there, because I'm mesmerized next by his tattoos. Sunbursts and tribal bands curl over his sinewy arms, and I'd like to lick them. I'd like to know if he's inked elsewhere and how far, or how low, the artwork on his body descends.

To his hips? The top of his ass? The V of his abs?

A woman can dream.

With a tilt of his head and a far-too-knowing grin, he answers, "Let me guess. You either didn't realize it, or you have someplace *real important* to be?"

"So important. I have to . . ." I trail off then make my voice as husky as can be as I set down my avocado, ". . . make guacamole."

"You don't say," he rasps, his low baritone caressing me all over. "I could help you with that, officer."

"Are you Mr. Avocado Farmer?"

"I'm Mr. I Can Show You How Ripe They Are." He steps into the booth, moving next to me, getting into my space.

Closer than he needs to be.

A tremble rolls over my shoulders as he crowds me. "Let's see." He strokes his neat beard, and I rein in a whimper. I want my hands on that scruff.

He studies the sea of avocados, reaching for one at last and then sliding even closer, so his shoulder touches mine. It's the match to my kindling and strikes a fire inside me.

If anyone tried to tell me a woman doesn't have a type, I'd call that person a liar.

I have a type, and the type lights me up from sea to shining sea.

He cups the fruit in his palm, then brings it near my chest. I draw a quick breath, then flick my hair off my shoulders.

"By the way," he says, "I like your hair up, but I fucking love it down."

Dead.

I am dead from desire.

Before I can reply—I'm honestly not sure I can form intelligible words—he rubs his other hand over the rind. "See, you want to find the one that's ripe and"—he pauses and turns his face to meet my gaze, his dark eyes holding mine—"ready to eat."

A shudder hijacks my body. "Is that so?"

I don't need a tutorial in picking avocados. Please. I know how to pick them just fine.

But I want his lesson. Want to hear his voice. Watch those hands move. Feel him slide closer.

"It'll feel slightly soft, and it'll yield to just the right amount of gentle pressure."

And that pressure builds between my legs, an insistent throb. "How do you tell if it's enough pressure?"

He pushes a thumb against the flesh of the fruit, making a husky hum low in his throat. "Just like that. See how it responds?"

"How's it responding?"

He turns, angling his body nearer to me, his dark eyes shining with desire as he roams them over my face, my hair, my breasts. "Just the way I like it."

This man is going to ruin me in the best possible way.

While I don't have the time or inclination for dating, dinners, or fitting someone into my very busy schedule, I'm pretty sure I could deal with a little ruination.

Yes, I could definitely do with getting ruined.

7
DEREK

Today is my lucky day.

I'd like to thank my sister for getting my ass out of bed.

I'd like to thank my niece for telling me the nice lady with the paints had just made her way down the veggie aisle.

And I'd like to thank fate that this avocado stand is in an out-of-the-way corner of the market, and that the farmer running it must have had to take one hell of a leak.

It's just us.

This woman is fiery, flirty, and already driving me out of my mind. The stream of market-goers has thinned to a crawl as we near closing time, and left us in a cocoon of raw lust.

I place the fruit on the red-and-white-checkered tablecloth, brush my fingers over her hip, and tug her against me. She lets out the sexiest little sound. "Tell me your name. I'm dying to know."

"Why do you need it so badly?"

"So I know what name to say when I'm fantasizing."

A murmur crosses her lips, and she leans her head back against me, her hair spilling down my chest. "Are you fantasizing about me?"

"Every. Single. Night."

"You must be having a lot of long nights, Mr. Trouble."

"Long, hard nights . . . Miss Demeanor," I say with a smirk, trying that nickname on for size.

"Well played."

"Thank you. It just came to me."

She glances back at me, her green eyes looking rife with dirty thoughts. "Do you want to *come* down to the station with me?"

"I want your name, beautiful. Give me your name," I growl into her ear, commanding her.

"Perri," she says breathlessly, her voice betraying her longing. A longing that matches mine.

"Perri," I repeat, tasting her name on my tongue.

Her voice tightens to a warning and sharpens as she speaks. "Don't say it."

I narrow my brow in question. "Say what?"

"Don't say it's a guy's name."

I laugh lightly in her ear, jerking her ass closer to my hard-on. "Do you honestly believe I'm thinking for one second about guys right now?"

She lets out a gasp, chased by a soft moan. "I don't know. What exactly are you thinking about?"

I drag my scruff against her neck. "How close I am to getting a ticket for indecent everything."

She wriggles her sexy rear against me. "I'd say everything feels way more than decent."

I groan as a dart of lust shoots down my spine. I'd like to find a way to kiss the breath out of her right here, right now.

She tenses against me, her body straightening like a ruler, and my gaze flicks to the new crowd of people streaming around the corner, heading toward us.

Fuck me.

She twists around, and I'm staring at her stunning face and lips that look like they desperately need to be kissed.

I tuck a finger under her chin. "Nothing indecent about touching your gorgeous face."

"No, I suppose it's not indecent at all."

"When are you done? I need to see you."

"You *need* to see me?" she challenges.

My gaze travels up and down her curves, noting the rise and fall of her shoulders, the flush in her cheeks, the parting of her lips. "Absolutely. And it goes both ways, I'd say. I need to see you, get my hands on you. And you need to be kissed so fucking hard that you stop sassing me."

A grin takes over her lips as she grabs two avocados—the one she touched and the one I was holding. "What makes you think a kiss would get me to stop sassing you?"

I smile back, shaking my head. "You're right. Why would I think you'd stop dishing it right back at me?"

"I think you like how I dish it."

"I believe you know I fucking love it." I reach for her belt loop. "Now listen, Perri. I'm done helping my sister in thirty minutes, and the way I see it is we can either grab a cup of coffee and gab about favorite TV shows and movies, then go for a stroll along the river and talk about what we do and where we went to college . . ." I quirk an eyebrow and lower my voice. "Or we can meet someplace where we can finish what the avocados started."

She nibbles on the corner of those sexy lips—lips I intend to get to know biblically well—and then lifts a hand and grabs the neck of my T-shirt, jerking me closer. "My friend runs the waffle truck on the outskirts of the market. Meet me there. I'm entering a kissing contest for charity, and if you can blow my mind in thirty minutes, you'll be my partner. That's your mission, should you choose to accept it."

I shake my head like a dog shucking off water.

A kissing contest? What the hell? I'd like a fucking contest, thank you very much. But fucking starts with kissing, so there's no earthly way I'm turning this chance down.

"Are you auditioning other candidates?"

With a sultry, confident stare, she shakes her head. "No. I'm waiting for you to blow me away."

"Funny. I was waiting for you to blow me away."

Her eyes take a tour of my body, stopping at my crotch. "We'll see about that."

I grab her wrist, grip her hand. "No one else is going to be kissing you in any contest, or by any waffle truck. Got that?"

"I guess you need to prove you have what it takes to make my knees weak."

"And your panties wet."

She wiggles an eyebrow, dips her face close, her soft cheek brushing against mine, and whispers in my ear, "You've already done that."

Then she tosses a five-dollar bill to the farmer, who must have returned at some point, says, "Thanks, Bob," and walks away.

Unabashedly, I tilt my head to the side, staring as she saunters down the aisle, giving me the chance to enjoy the sight of her ass, so fucking spectacular in those jeans.

As surreptitiously as possible, I adjust myself, then a pang of guilt stabs me.

We just practically dry-fucked in Farmer Bob's stand. The least I can do is pay for the privilege. I buy a bag of avocados and hope to hell someone in the house wants guacamole.

By the time the market ends, guac is the last thing on my mind.

The waffle truck is first and foremost.

8

DEREK

Thirty interminable minutes later, I make my way to the food truck, eager to see her again. Maybe we're going to don aprons and hats and whip up Belgian waffles, an entrée to the main course of kissing that would also go well with whipped cream and strawberries.

But I don't want to play patty-cake drop-a-dollop-of-whipped-cream-on-your-nose-and-get-to-know-you games. I'm not interested in dating, and I don't have the bandwidth to fit that in—not on top of the new job and taking care of my family.

Those are my priorities, and there's no room for anything else.

But I do like the idea of kissing the taste of strawberries and whipped cream off Perri's sweet, pouty lips.

When I reach the truck, a CLOSED placard is perched at the window, and I curse.

But a second later, my red-haired beauty appears at the window, leaning over the steel edge, wiping a waffle crumb off her lips, a hint of mischief in her green eyes.

"So sorry, sir. The truck is closed." Her tone is the definition of coy.

I lift an eyebrow. "What if I'm not here for the waffles?"

"Interesting," she says, taking her time with the word. "Whatever would you be here for, then?"

"I believe I'm here for the one-fifteen appointment to prove I can make your knees weak."

A naughty smile is my reward, then she glances down, checking out an invisible schedule. She taps the imaginary page with a finger. "Why, yes. I do see you, right here. But I have one question."

"Hit me."

She bends closer in the window, resting her chin in her palm. "Do you like sweet or savory?"

I take a beat before I answer. "I have a healthy appetite for . . . *everything*. But I especially love to eat sweet things." I reach for a strand of her hair, twisting it in my fingers. "Sweet red things."

A gust of breath seems to cross her lips, then she whispers, "I need to warn you. My lips might taste like cucumber and tomatoes."

"I'd be open to taste-testing."

"Then I'm open to your appointment." She leans over the edge of the window, those tits pushing up in her white T-shirt, sending my dick speeding into full-speed arousal. This is when she should give me a ticket —semi to flagpole in less than a second.

This woman is a temptress like I've never seen before.

I stare at her, my jaw tight, my desire already stoked high. I exhale sharply. "Open the fucking door to the waffle truck, Perri."

A little murmur tells me she likes the command, and it also makes me curious if she's the kind of woman who's so used to giving orders and telling people what to do all damn day that she likes a few orders in the sack.

"Come around to the back," she whispers.

I peer inside the window, confirming the truck is empty. Only her. I head to the back, and she's there holding the door open.

She slides a finger over her lips. "Listen." Her tone turns serious. "My friend Staci took off for about ten minutes to pick up her regular grocery order from the farmers. No one can see us in here, but we don't have—"

I drop my head, claim her mouth, and shut her up with a kiss. A hard, punishing, powerful kiss for a woman who seems to want it that way.

"Oh God," she gasps into my mouth, looping her arms around my neck. We crash against the wall next to the sink, utensils clattering. She yanks me closer, and we claim each other.

There's no prelude, no buildup. Just kissing at sixty miles an hour. Pure need and adrenaline. Heat jolts down my spine. A wild storm of lust surges in my gut.

I grind against her, letting her feel my length, letting her know I'm so goddamn ready to go.

Push. Grind. Press.

She responds to every move with a tighter grip around my neck, with her fingers lacing around my head, with a sharp tug on the ends of my hair.

She's so fucking fiery. Maybe I'm wrong about her liking orders. But I want to find out every little detail about what turns this woman on.

Or turns her on even more. Judging from her moans and whimpers, she's already on a fast track to the pleasure zone.

She breaks the kiss and slides a hand down my shirt, dancing over my abs, setting me alight. Her hand reaches the outline of my dick, cupping me. "That feels way more than decent," she purrs.

I lean my head back and groan. A feral, filthy groan. Because this woman is going to kill me with lust. She's in my head and under my skin, and I want her more than I want world peace, and hey, I'd really like world peace.

But I'd also like to fuck Perri and make her come again and again. I'd like this truck to be rocking. "I promise you will feel indecent, incredible, indescribable pleasure when I get you naked and under me, above me, and bent over."

She squeezes harder. "I see you've already picked out a wide selection of positions."

I drop my mouth to hers and bite the corner of her lips. She yelps, then presses her pelvis against me, the perfect angle for friction. "And I see you're trying to get a piece of my cock right now," I growl.

Her lips open in a startled O. "I'm going to have to arrest you for filthy language."

I shake my head and plant a hard, bruising kiss on her pretty mouth. "I think you like filthy language."

"I think I like what you're doing to me," she murmurs and slides her hands around my hips to my ass, squeezing it.

I bend to her again, capturing those pouty lips once more in a searing kiss. I consume her mouth, sweeping my tongue across hers and savoring the flavor of her kiss. I don't taste tomatoes and cucumber. I taste salt and desire. I taste the sweetness of a hint of gloss. And I smell her want. I fucking inhale her lust. It's heady and intoxicating, swirling around me, and it makes me want to drag her back to my—

Fuck. There's no "my place" to go to.

So I kiss her impossibly harder since this is not a woman who likes slow. The thought makes me laugh.

I chuckle as I kiss her, and she slams her hands against my pecs. "What's so funny about kissing me, Mr. Speedy?"

"I was just thinking how I could give you a ticket for kissing too fast."

"You don't like the way I kiss?"

I laugh again, grab her hand, and bring it back to my shaft. "Kitten, I'm so fucking turned on that you're going to have to lock me in this waffle truck for an hour for my dick to go down. I love everything about the way you kiss. I love that you're not a slow kisser. I love that you're ferocious and fiery." I slide her hand down my length, watching as her eyes go hazy. "I love that you're as ready for this as I am."

"Do you think I'm wound up?" Her voice is breathy as she strokes me.

"I bet your panties are soaked and you're aching between your legs."

She whimpers, then grabs my jaw and slams my mouth back to hers. "Kiss me hard."

"As if I'd do anything else."

I do as the lady asks, devouring her sweet mouth. Our teeth click, our tongues lash, and our breath comes in fast, sharp pants.

I grind against her, and she grinds right back. I half wonder why we're not fucking right now, but I also have enough brains to know she's a cop, and even if this truck is on the edge of the market, and even if we're out of sight, she's still a bit of a public figure.

But that doesn't stop me from letting my fingers wander. They slide down her body, over her belly, and to the waistband of her jeans. I slip a hand under her shirt, feeling the soft flesh of her stomach.

"You feel so fucking good." I unbutton the top button on her jeans.

Her hand darts out, stopping me. "*Derek.*"

Her tone is 100 percent warning. I heed it, stopping. "What is it?"

"If your hand goes any farther south, I'm going to fuck your fingers."

My mind officially goes haywire, wires tripping, nerve endings fraying, my brain combusting. "That's the sexiest thing anyone's ever said in the history of the world."

"But we can't. We have to stop."

I nod, getting it, even as my cock and fingers have other ideas. I cup her jaw. "How did I do with my appointment? Did I pass?"

Her lips quirk. "With flying colors. The only question now is what category we're going to enter in."

"There are categories?"

Her green eyes dance. "Oh yes. Sweetest, most passionate, best reenactment. I'm not sure which one would be best."

I thread a hand through her hair. "We should practice again. Meet me later."

"Like on a date?" Her tone drips with skepticism, and I believe I've met my non-dating soul mate.

I laugh. "Sounds like you're about as interested in dating as I am."

She nods fiercely. "Yes, as in zero."

"Good, because relationships aren't my thing these days."

"That makes two of us."

"And we don't need to date to practice for your contest."

"We absolutely don't." She taps her chin, her eyes drifting to a clipboard on the wall. "Let's see. The contest is in three weeks. We could practice again, say, Thursday night?"

"That's a long time from now."

She laughs. "Good. You'll be even readier then. How about you pick a time and place and text me?"

She is my kind of woman. Confident. Bold. Plays zero games. "But make it good, Derek McHotPants."

"It won't be good, kitten. It'll be oh so fucking good your toes will curl."

"I can't wait."

She enters her number into my phone, pecks a kiss to my lips, then kicks me out.

I've never been so happy to be shown the door.

9

PERRI

"Check this out," Shaw declares proudly.

At the grill on our parents' deck that evening, my brother stands next to my father, sliding a spatula under a hamburger.

Dad rolls his hazel eyes. "You're not going to do this *again*, are you?"

Shaw nods vigorously as he waggles the burger-laden spatula. "Don't you trust me, Dad?"

Dad huffs. "It's not that I don't trust you. It's that I absolutely don't trust you for a hot second not to mess up the most fantastic burgers I've made this year."

Shaw claps Dad on the shoulder—they're the same height and have been since Shaw was in high school. Six foot forever. Same build too—big. Same sense of humor—sarcastic as hell.

"Dad, I don't want to hear that kind of negative self-talk. All your burgers are incredible. Say it with me." Shaw puffs out his chest and adopts a Stuart

Smalley tone. "My burgers are good enough, and gosh darn it, people like them."

"What did I do to deserve this kind of torture?" Dad grabs another spatula and tries to swat Shaw's burger back onto the grill. I watch from my spot in the Adirondack chair on the deck. Shaw-and-Dad slapstick is the best spectator theater. I lean closer to Vanessa, whispering, "Bet you've never seen this routine before."

"Never," she says sarcastically. "But it never grows old."

Shaw darts around Dad and grabs another burger.

"You deserve this, Sam. You taught him everything he knows about being a provocateur," Mom calls out through the open kitchen window.

"I did not, Gail."

"Oh yes you did, and now it's payback time," she says.

Shaw turns to Vanessa and me. "Place your bets, ladies. Will the juggler and star of the firemen calendar crush it at burger flipping, or will he *absolutely* crush it like no one has crushed it before?"

Vanessa cups the side of her mouth. "The judges haven't ruled. We want to see what you can do first."

"Behold." Shaw fixes his eyes on Vanessa in her capri jeans and short-sleeve summer sweater. With the spatula, he tosses the first burger high in the air then whacks the next one skyward. As they fly, he wiggles an eyebrow, winking as he catches the first grilled burger on the spatula, then the second. He slides them back on the grill, holds his arms out wide, and takes a triumphant bow.

Vanessa claps. "And the judges have voted you on to the next round."

"Hey, I'm on the jury too. I never vote in his favor," I chime in.

Shaw turns to Dad. "See, Dad? And you never believed I had talent."

Dad laughs again. "I always believed you had plenty of talent. That's why I figured you'd join the big top rather than the fire service."

"There's still time," I shout. "I heard the circus is having tryouts for clowns in a week."

Vanessa provides a rim shot on an invisible drum set. "Hey Shaw, just how many burgers can you juggle?"

Dad swivels around, waving his spatula like a weapon. "Don't encourage him or you'll be banished, and I always liked you."

Vanessa adopts the sweetest smile. "Of course, Mr. Keating. I won't feed the circus animals anymore."

We're at our parents' house for our usual Sunday supper. When Shaw and I aren't on shifts, we come here every week and our parents treat us—and sometimes our friends too—to a feast, as we share the latest on jobs and life. Mom's a former firefighter, one of the few female former chiefs in the state, and Dad's a retired prosecutor. The apples didn't fall far from the tree with Shaw and me.

Shaw darts through the open door to the kitchen and returns seconds later with a ketchup bottle, a mustard container, and some steak sauce, sending the three bottles spinning in the air.

Dad groans, but Vanessa cheers him on. "Higher! Higher!"

He does as he's asked, a fierce look of concentration in his hazel eyes, and I swear he's performing for her. Well, that's not a surprise. Men tend to perform for women. Even if he's known her for years, and Vanessa is practically our sister. Guys always try to impress the chicks.

"What else can you juggle?" Vanessa asks, as he sets the condiments on the deck railing.

Shaw scans the porch when Mom calls out, "Don't even think about juggling plates, Shaw."

He holds up his hands in innocence. "Who? Me?" To Vanessa, he says, "I can juggle pretty much anything. As soon as you get the hang of it, all you have to do is know the rhythm and keep it as you toss."

"Can you, say, juggle bowling balls?" she challenges.

"Vanessa, do not let this trickster convince you that he can juggle bowling balls," I warn.

"I just want to see if Shaw will try to convince me that it's actually possible. Or really, if he can convince himself."

He smiles at her. "I'll have you know, I am a most excellent convincer. In fact, I have received a master's degree in convincing."

Mom pokes her head out onto the deck, using her best battalion chief voice. "All right, master convincer, why don't you bring my ketchup, mustard, and steak sauce back inside, so I don't have to convince you the hard way to set the table?"

"Yes, ma'am."

We head inside and mingle in the kitchen, grabbing drinks and chatting before gathering at the table a little later when Gabe and Arden arrive. As we sit down to eat, Mom clears her throat. "Vanessa, can you say grace? I always love how you say it."

"Of course, Mrs. Keating." Vanessa says thank you for the dinner in Spanish, her first language. She's fluent in both Spanish and English, since she moved here from Colombia when she was six.

"Beautiful," Mom says.

Shaw nods, echoing, "Beautiful."

We dig into the meal, enjoying the salad, burgers, and corn as Mom quizzes my friends on what they're up to these days, even though she saw the full crew only two weeks ago.

Arden tells a story about a book club she's been hosting at the store, and Gabe catches my parents up on how his grandpa is doing—he's holding on well enough.

Dad lifts a glass of water. "Sometimes 'well enough' is all you can wish for. I'll drink a toast to that."

"Me too," Gabe says.

"And Shaw, how are you feeling about Charlie having moved away?" my mother asks, referring to the paramedic he was close with. Recently, Charlie returned to his hometown in Florida.

"Well, I miss the bastard." Shaw brings the burger to his mouth and takes a bite.

Mom gives him a look. "Language." She might have once hung out in the boy's club at the firehouse, but that doesn't mean she talked the dirty talk with them. "Why can't you just say, 'I miss my friend'?"

Gabe lifts his chin. "I can do it, Mrs. Keating." He glances at Shaw. "Watch how it's done." Gabe takes a deep breath. "I miss my friend."

Mom smiles, satisfied, gesturing to Gabe, then Shaw. "See?"

Shaw chews then huffs. "Fine, Mom. I miss the guy. But there's a new guy who took his place, and he's cool, so it'll be fine."

Mom smiles. "It's always nice to make new friends."

"Yes," I chime in, "isn't it wonderful after all this time that Shaw is finally playing well with the other boys?"

Mom stares at me. "Are you being sassy, missy?"

"Hmm. Am I?" I pretend to think about it. "Definitely," I answer.

"And is sass the way to win a promotion?" Mom counters.

"I'm not sassy with the chief," I say sheepishly.

"Then don't be sassy with me."

"Yes, ma'am."

Arden grabs the conversational steering wheel. "Speaking of, what do you think about the new promotion that Perri's up for, Mr. and Mrs. Keating? I'm so excited about the possibility."

I cross my fingers. "Let's hope it happens. I want it so badly."

"All you have to do is be the friendly face of the department, keep up your impeccable record at busting scofflaws, and oh, what's the last one?" Arden asks playfully.

Vanessa waggles her arms excitedly. "Oh, I know, I know! Call on me, please!"

I roll my eyes. "Seriously, guys?"

Arden points to Vanessa. "You want to do the honors?"

Dad sets down his burger, his hazel eyes curious. "This I'd like to hear."

"Me too," Mom says. "What's going on now?"

Vanessa points animatedly at me. "Her boss wants her to enter a kissing contest."

Dad arches a brow. "That one in Whiskey Hollows?"

"Oh my God, is everyone doing this contest?" I ask.

Mom gives Dad a flirty look, and I drop my forehead into my palm. "Please, dear God, please oh please tell me my parents aren't doing the contest."

But when I look up, they're already lip-locked. He's leaned next to her and is planting a big fat kiss on her lips.

Gabe whistles while Arden cheers and Shaw shouts, "Get a room."

They break apart, and Mom bats her lashes. "We've still got it."

"And I'm still going to need therapy," I tease.

"Oh, please. I've always believed the best example that parents can set is to show appropriate physical affection in front of their children. Now, who's your kissing partner? Also, don't even think you can beat us in the seniors category."

I crack up. "You're right, Mom. I can't best you there."

She squeezes my dad's arm then turns her focus back to me. "So, who is he? Have you met someone? Is there a new guy?"

"Please. I have no time for dating or relationships," I say, though the truth is a little sadder. Men don't ask me out much. It's a power thing. Being a cop can intimidate people, so my dating life has been woefully limited to men I've met online, and I've simply never found a meaningful connection there. I affect my best carefree smile. "But who needs a relationship? I only need a kissing partner for the contest. I'm helping raise money for first responders."

I flash back over the early afternoon kiss at the waffle truck. The shake-the-earth, rock-me-to-my-core, turn-me-inside-out-with-pleasure kiss. The can-it-please-be-Thursday-so-I-can-sneak-off-and-do-it-again kiss. A fresh wave of sensation curls through my body, warming me up. I try to shuck it off, since I do not need to get retroactively aroused at the dinner table. But damn, that man can kiss like a rock star. And I bet that man can do everything in bed like a rock star too.

"And you have a kissing partner," Arden says, suggestively.

"She totally found someone to enter with," Vanessa seconds.

Shaw laughs as he takes another bite of his burger, chuckling at me. "This I'm dying to know. I thought you were basically undatable, sis."

I give him a sneer and a kick under the table. *In the shin.* He cringes, but quickly rearranges his features into his best stoic face.

Dad tsks. "Perri, do you really have to do that?"

I shrug, like the innocent I am. "Do what?"

"I know you kicked your brother under the table."

"Can you blame me? Would you actually prosecute that, considering the mitigating circumstances—those being that Shaw is acting just like Shaw?"

Dad laughs. "Son, behave. Can you do that for me?"

Shaw sighs heavily, like it takes a ton of effort. "I don't know that I ever have. Should I really start now?"

"You know what they say, Mr. Keating," Gabe chimes in. "Can't teach an old dog new tricks, and Shaw is most definitely an old dog."

Shaw barks, then he turns to me. "Anyway, you haven't dated anybody in the longest time. Do you have a secret lover? A brand-new beau? A hot new piece of man meat on the side?"

My mother heaves the most dramatic sigh in the universe.

Shaw holds up his hands in surrender. "Sorry, Mom."

I stare at my brother. "Seriously, how have you ever had a girlfriend? How is that even possible?"

Vanessa coughs then stares purposefully at her plate. I shoot her a quizzical look but return my focus to my brother. "Seriously, Shaw. Man meat?"

"So, who is the man meat, and do I need to beat him up?"

I laugh, because even though he's a complete pain in the ass, I do love his crazy-protective side. "No, you don't need to beat him up. He's . . ." My voice trails off, and I'm not entirely sure what I want to tell them. I go with the simplest of details. "He's focused and determined, and he has these sunburst tattoos all the way up his arm."

"Ooh," Mom says, squeezing Dad's arm. "I've always loved the inked ones."

Dad eyes his unmarked arm. "Does that mean you want me to go out and get a tattoo, Gail?"

Her eyes darken. "No, dear, I don't think it would suit you."

"You don't?"

"I'm kidding. Could you get one across your chest? Make sure to put my name in it."

"Count on it," he says then drops a kiss on her cheek.

"You two are so in love it's kind of gross, except it's totally awesome," I say.

Gabe and Arden raise their glasses, and Arden adds, "It's thoroughly awesome."

Mom looks to me. "Tell us more about your kissing partner. What's he like?"

He's a filthy, fantastic, hot-as-sin lover. He likes to flirt and kiss and tease, and drive me out of my mind with pleasure. He's cocky, confident, and knows what he wants. He wants *me*.

But none of that is for public consumption. I spear a bite of tomato in the salad, hold it up, and give them a PG version. "His name is Derek, and he kisses like the only person I could ever imagine kissing in a kissing contest."

Shaw makes a sound like a laugh met a cough, sputtering in amusement. "Seriously?"

I stare at him curiously. "Yes, what's so weird about that?"

"Nothing," he says, his expression instantly turning serious. "That's just epic."

Vanessa laughs. "Why is that epic?"

"That is the best thing I've ever heard."

"Why?" I press.

Shaw smiles sweetly, reminding me there's a good guy underneath his constant desire to needle me. We might drive each other crazy, but we love each other like mad and look out for each other as only family can. "I'm just excited you've found somebody you can picture kissing for that long."

"Thank you, Shaw. I never thought I'd hear you say such a nice thing. But yes, I do think more practice will indeed help."

"Practice makes perfect," he adds.

"See? Isn't it nicer when the two of you get along?" Mom asks.

Shaw nods. "I'll have you know I'm a very nice

brother. If memory serves, I'm helping you rent the room above your garage."

I soften more. "I don't know what I'd do without you. You're incredibly helpful. And I love to give you a hard time, but you're actually the best brother a girl could ask for. You're a Neanderthal sometimes, but other times you're quite civilized and sweet."

Shaw grins. "And Perri, you're a pain in the ass—"

"Language," Mom chides.

"But you're super awesome too," he adds.

I smile at him. "Super awesome and civilized. See how great we get along?"

Shaw grins. "In fact, I think you're going to be amazed at how civilized I am."

10

DEREK

At the Barking Pug that night, Shaw raises two fingers to catch the bartender's attention then turns to me. "Drinks are on me."

"Thanks, man. I appreciate it."

The mustached bartender slaps down two napkins. "What can I get you?"

"Two beers. Whatever's good on tap."

"Got an IPA tonight that you'll like, Shaw," the guy says.

"That work for you?" Shaw asks.

I drum my fingers against the scratched wood surface of the bar. "I'm one hundred percent not picky about beer."

"I'll drink to that."

The beers arrive, and Shaw thanks the bartender then slaps some bills on the counter. "So what do you think of our small town so far?" He raises his glass to take a drink.

I swallow some of the beer. "Can't complain. The people here are great," I say, flashing back to the market yesterday, and yeah, I'm thinking of Perri, but I'm also thinking of all the people I met while working my sister's baked goods booth.

"Yeah? Have you met a lot of folks yet?"

"Definitely. At the market yesterday, a lot of my sister's regulars were welcoming, asking me questions, wondering if I needed anything, could they help, et cetera."

Shaw cocks a brow. "That so?"

I laugh lightly. "Does that surprise you?"

"Were they, by chance, female?"

I picture the long line of volunteers yesterday then concede his point. "Fine, most were."

"Were they interested in helping you find your way to the hardware store or sort out your utility bill, or was it making sure you don't get snatched up by some other lady in town first?"

"If that's what they were after, it'd be a losing cause."

"Why's that?"

I tap my chest. "Single as the day is long."

He regards me quizzically. "Does that mean you're single and have a parade of ladies at your door every night?"

"No way. I mean, not that there's anything wrong with that. But that's not my style. Besides, I've been pretty damn busy with work and taking care of my nieces and nephew."

"That's good of you to help out with them."

"I love those rug rats. Molly, Devon, and Travis are fucking awesome. And my sister's the best. We were always close, but after our parents died a few years ago, we've been even tighter."

"Sorry to hear about your parents."

"Thanks, but honestly, it wasn't a big surprise. They were in their late seventies. They were older when they had us. My mom was forty-one when Jodie was born and forty-six when I surprised them both."

"Damn, that's impressive."

"It is, but I still won't be imitating them. I don't plan on procreating any time soon."

"I will definitely drink to that," Shaw says, and we tip our glasses.

"To keeping it wrapped up."

He's quiet for a minute, like he's thinking of something. I'm not one to break the silence, especially since a ball game is on and the bases are loaded. When the batter flies out, Shaw returns to the conversation. "Think you're going to take any of those ladies from your sister's booth up on their offers to"—he sketches air quotes—"*help?*"

I laugh, shaking my head. "Nah, I'm not interested in dating right now either."

"I hear you. Relationships can be a bitch."

"Especially after my last one," I say, darkly.

"Yeah?"

"She was bad news."

"What's the story there? Or is it an I'd-rather-not-say thing?"

I appreciate the dude giving me space not to say

anything about it. "Let's just say we had different ideas of commitment. I believed in one-on-one, and she believed it was a multitiered approach involving other people."

"Ouch."

I wave a hand. "It was all for the best in the end. But it left me with a bad taste in my mouth."

A bitter taste, considering how things went south with Katie, my live-in girlfriend, a couple of years ago.

I give him the bare-bones version.

We shared a place in San Francisco and had an ironclad lease for a year.

Trouble was, she had an ironclad interest in the building's new landlord.

One day I forgot my lunch, and since we'd just finished a call in the neighborhood, I had my partner stop the rig at our place. I ran upstairs, planning to duck inside, grab my lunch bag from the fridge, and go.

Instead, I found Katie on the kitchen table. The landlord was between her legs, having her for lunch.

Yeah, that was fun.

Moving out and finding a new place was even less fun.

Since then, my interest in getting serious has dwindled to less than zero.

The only solace was he jacked her rent through the roof when she dumped him a few months later. I heard through the grapevine that she couldn't afford to stay and had to move into a one-bedroom with six other people, or something like that.

I take another drink of my beer then set it down. "Anyway, that's one of the reasons why I'm single. I don't have time for that shit in my life right now."

He nods, seemingly pleased with my answer. He scratches his jaw. "Listen, I know you're looking for a place. I didn't mention this sooner because I had a few loose ends to tie up, but I have a room above the garage for you. Separate entrance and everything. It even has its own bathroom. Plus, it's less than a mile from your sister's house."

That piques my interest. Shaw's a good guy, and I wouldn't mind sharing space with him. I doubt we'd run into each other too much, but if we did, it'd be cool.

He shows me some pics on his phone, and it's a sweet, spacious finished room above the garage.

Ten minutes later, I'm buying the next round—soda this time, since we both need to drive—and toasting.

He emails me the agreement, and I give my digital John Hancock, initiating a transfer for the first month's rent. Nothing too fancy in the lease. Just a standard rental arrangement. The best part? Well, the second-best part, after the bed? It's month by month, and that suits me fine.

I raise a glass to Shaw. "This helps so fucking much."

All he had to say was "king-size bed above the garage," and I was sold.

Shaw shakes his head. "Nope. It's the least I can do."

When we finish, we head out of the Barking Pug, and he follows me as I ride to my sister's. I park the bike there, figuring I'll pick it up tomorrow, then I toss a duffel into the back of Shaw's truck, and we drive the mile to his home.

It's . . . well, much prettier than I'd pictured.

A porch swing hangs in the front. The deck is lined with potted plants. Flowers bloom in the front yard. I lift a brow as I spot a mailbox decorated with drawings of envelopes and stationery in every shade of pastel.

Shaw's taste is . . . unexpected.

We walk along a well-kept stone path to the front porch where a doormat shaped like a watermelon greets our feet.

"This is, um, cute."

He nods. "Yeah, my sister has good taste."

He presses the doorbell, and I tilt my head to the side, asking, "Sister?"

Gesturing to the lawn, he answers, "Yeah. It's her place. I help her rent the room above the garage. But don't worry. There's plenty of privacy, and she's cool. Well, as long as you don't break the law."

I tense, wondering what he means.

But the answer is crystal clear when the door opens, and standing there is the law-enforcing someone I had my lips all over yesterday.

11

PERRI

I answer the door at eight at night in my orange-and-black witch-patterned pajama bottoms, a spaghetti strap tank, and a messy bun. I haven't done laundry in a week, and the Halloween jammies are the only ones clean. But the washing machine is running right now, so there's that Pyrrhic victory.

Also for the record, I'm sporting zero makeup and zero support for the girls.

Braless for the . . . *not win?*

Exactly what I don't want to be wearing when I see Derek McHotPants again.

I furrow my brow, staring at the sight on my doorstep—a satisfied Shaw, a confused Derek, and a duffel bag. I'm thoroughly perplexed too. But hey, I've walked into meth houses a few towns over, run down thieves who've nicked five-hundred-dollar vintages of wine, and I've busted vagrants for harassing citizens.

My poker face is epic, from practice and from

necessity. I can absolutely handle the guy I want to bang six ways to Sunday showing up on my front porch next to my brother, of all people.

I lean against the doorway, doing my best *annoyed homeowner not wanting to deal with door-to-door salesmen*. "Are you selling magazines? Because my subscription to *Good Housekeeping* just ran out. But I'd love to re-up if you can give me a great deal."

There. That's the perfect counterpoint to my pajama couture.

Derek's lips quirk up. "Funny thing, I do in fact have magazine subscriptions, as well as Encyclopedia Britannica if you need them. But they come with a catch. You would need to order a couple dozen boxes of turtle clusters."

A smile threatens to break through my tough girl facade. "I guess it'll be a hard pass, then. I have never been a fan of turtle clusters."

Derek whispers, conspirator-style, "Me neither. I never understood how anyone could peddle those things."

Shaw spreads his arms wide, pleased as a dog lounging on laundry fresh and warm from the dryer. "See? That's what I'm talking about. This is going to be perfect."

What is he talking about? Because I'm still at a loss as to why either of them is here, unannounced. "What's going to be perfect?"

He smirks. It's the smirkiest smirk ever. Then he smacks his forehead. "My bad. Wherever are my manners? Perri, I did as you asked. I rented the room above the garage. To Derek."

I freeze. No. Just hell-to-the-no. He did not say *that*.

This has to be Shaw's idea of a joke.

This is my wisecracking, full-of-it brother. This is payback for . . . kicking his shin under the table? Though this hardly seems tit for tat.

"What did you just say?" I ask through my confusion.

Shaw is undeterred, gesturing grandly to the man next to him. "Derek, meet Perri. If you ever get scared, she'll protect you. She sleeps with her piece."

I raise my hands in exasperation. "One, I do not. Two, what the hell, Shaw? Is this another one of your jokes?"

He's dead serious. "No. Why?"

Derek gulps but wisely keeps his mouth closed.

I stare at my brother. "Seriously? I asked you to rent the room. I didn't ask you to rent it to . . ." I trail off—I have no idea how I should refer to Derek.

Lover seems like a massive overstep. He's not earned that title yet, even if I want to slam it on him as much as I'd wanted him to slam me against the steel wall of the waffle truck yesterday.

My *about-to-be hookup*?

That sounds rather gauche.

A screw toy? Fuck fling? A coming-soon-to-a-one-night-stand-near-you?

Shaw clears his throat and speaks confidently, like

that kid in school who's sure he has the right answer. "You wanted me to rent the room, and I did. To a responsible, respectable, cool-as-fuck dude who desperately needs a place to stay while he's in town to help out his sister and her kids, who happen to live down the street from you. Is that what you meant to say, Perri?"

I fume, squeezing my eyes shut, gritting my teeth.

When I open my eyes, Derek is laughing. But it sounds forced. "Hey, no worries. I thought Shaw lived here. Listen, it's fine."

Shaw beams. "Exactly. It's all fine. This is the ideal solution. You wanted a renter. Derek's a good guy. He's not going to bang anyone else. You're not going to bang anyone else. Neither one of you wants a relationship. It's the absolute perfect rental situation. You can work on your kissing practice to win that contest, and he can be near his sis. Admit it—this is a brilliant solution."

He's serious.

There's no hint of a ruse. No secret smile underneath it all. He's not playing some sort of joke on me, because when he does, Shaw usually breaks under pressure quickly.

He's not breaking. He's not bending either. Carefully, I ask my brother, "You planned this after I told you about him at dinner yesterday?"

Derek, brow furrowed in a frown, cuts in. "It's okay, Perri. Don't worry about it. I can find another place to stay."

And all I can figure is he's annoyed I mentioned

him to my brother at all. Come to think of it, I'd probably be annoyed too.

Shaw jumps in. "Listen, I need to jet. I'm meeting Gabe at the gym. But be nice to each other. Remember, the key to being good roomies is respect, tolerance, and privacy."

Shaw hauls me in for a big brotherly hug. "It's going to be great. Aren't you proud of me for being helpful?"

"Pride is not the dominant emotion I'm feeling right now," I deadpan.

If we were alone, I'd give him a piece of my mind. I'd give him a full serving, plus a second helping of *are you fucking insane?*

Shaw tips his imaginary hat. "Looks like my work is done." He wipes one hand against the other, trots down the steps, gets into his truck, and peels away.

Leaving me standing in the doorway looking at the man I want to jump.

The man who's my new . . . housemate?

12

PERRI

I'm obviously an asshole.

But still.

Am I truly supposed to rent the room above my garage to this . . . specimen?

Yes, that's exactly the word I was searching for.

Derek is an exemplary specimen of a man. All inked, muscled, tall, dark, and handsome, crooked-grinned man. With a square jaw to boot, deliciously covered in a neat, trim beard I want to feel against my inner thighs.

Fuck.

I am a dirty girl.

A bad, naughty vixen who objectifies too-hot-for-words men.

But seriously. The man radiates sex appeal. I bet cats everywhere rub their faces against his legs to mark him. The man was built for sex. He's the stuff of panty-melting ovary explosions.

Which means this is a predicament, since I have a bit of cat in me and I'd like to rub up against him.

Derek glances at the sidewalk, and for the first time since our encounter on the side of the road, his cocky veneer is stripped off. "Why don't I hit the road? I'll go back to my sister's house. This was obviously some sort of misunderstanding."

"Obviously," I say, but a sliver of guilt festers under my skin. "Because it's weird. Right? It would be weird if you were my housemate."

He nods quickly, reaching to pick up his bag. "Totally weird."

Then I recall Shaw's words. My brother actually said Derek and I could practice kissing. That means Derek doesn't simply know I mentioned him to Shaw —he knows I told Shaw about our kiss. Red spots of embarrassment flame across my cheeks. "Wait, Derek." I grab his arm before he picks up the bag. "I didn't tell him to find you and rent it to you. I didn't know you guys knew each other. Please don't think I was trying to trap you or anything."

He chuckles lightly. "You mean you aren't trying to trap me?"

"I'm so not trying to trap you. I'm trying to kick you out," I say, laughing, then I let go of his arm.

"I don't feel trapped, for what it's worth." He doesn't reach for the bag.

"I said something about entering a kissing contest with a guy who had sunburst tattoos," I say, my eyes straying to his arms. Dear God, his arms. I want to feel them pinning me down, to stare at them as he moves above me.

I shake my head, trying to snap out of it.

"You like my ink?" he asks.

"I do."

"I have more where that came from," he says in that low, deep voice that's an injection of pure liquid pleasure.

So is the vision he's painted—the idea that art covers his body in places I can't see right now. I try to wave off the wild images of his hips, his lower back, his abdomen. "Anyway, sorry about the misunderstanding. There wasn't a trap or plan. Shaw was just being Shaw."

"It's all good. I'll head back to Jodie's. There's a couch there calling my name." This time, he grabs his duffel and slings it over his shoulder. It looks like it weighs three hundred pounds.

I peer around for his bike, but don't see it. "You're going to walk back with all your stuff?"

"It's no big deal. It's good training for work."

I point to the bag. "Is that all you have?"

"Yeah, but listen, it's all good."

But it's not all good. It's all . . . weird. It's all awkward. And it's all so uncomfortable—for him.

The man is living on his sister's couch, out of a duffel.

I'm not heartless enough to kick him completely to the curb. "Why don't you come in, and we can talk. I'll try to help you figure something out. Do you like wine?"

His lips curve up. "Am I in trouble if I say no?"

I give him my best staring-down-perps stare. "It's illegal to dislike wine in wine country. You might, in fact, be banished from the town limits. By me."

He smiles. "Just messing with you, officer. Of course I like wine."

"Good answer, Mr. Trouble."

Winking, he enters and drops his bag on the floor in the entryway.

I head to the kitchen, gesturing for him to follow. As I glance quickly at my mostly neat living room, I'm reminded I wasn't expecting a man tonight. If I had known he was coming, I'd have done the Swiffer-duster dance, cleaning every surface, spraying the bathroom mirrors, putting away every container of deodorant or bottle of Midol to make sure he never knew I might possibly sweat or have PMS.

I'd have sidled up to the door, a touch of gloss on and something casual but sexy framing my figure.

Instead, I'm in jammies and wearing no face paint. There's no cosmetic artifice, but what do I have to hide anyway?

In the kitchen, he scans my collection of fridge magnets, which covers almost every square inch of the appliance. They're nearly all vintage-style pictures of women saying sarcastic things, courtesy of my retro-loving friend, Vanessa.

Yoga class? I thought you said pour another glass.

And I thought I wanted a career. Turns out I just wanted paychecks.

You piqued my indifference.

He smirks, tapping the last one. "Very you."

"Is it?"

"Full of sass and spark."

I smile. "You've got me there." I grab a bottle of chardonnay and a wine opener.

"Let me." He reaches for the bottle before I can say *I am woman, I can do it all.*

Watching him open the bottle also feeds my inner vixen. Is it my imagination or do those tattoos ripple when his muscles move?

I grab wineglasses and give them to him.

He pours and hands me a glass, raising his own. "Should we drink to good witches? Or bad witches?"

I look down at the ridiculous pattern on the pants. "We'll drink to Monday night laundry."

"And to simple misunderstandings?"

My heart pangs with guilt again as I take a sip. "I'm sorry. I can't believe he really thought that made sense to rent it to you."

"Don't think twice about it."

"You agree, right?"

"Of course."

"So we're on the same page," I say, pressing.

"Let me make one thing clear." He meets my gaze, his dark-brown eyes holding mine intently. "I had every intention of meeting you on Thursday night, kissing you senseless until your knees wobbled and your panties were so damn wet you had to come home to change. I'd have gotten you so goddamn riled up, you'd be squirming on your bed that night, aching and wet again, and call me, begging me to talk dirty to you till you came hard with your fingers."

Oh. My. God.

I'm officially a melted puddle of lust. Grab a mop, swab me up. I'm liquid, molten desire seeping across my kitchen floor.

I part my lips to speak, but a moan traitorously escapes instead.

A fucking moan.

I clamp my lips shut.

He arches a brow, his eyes saying he likes that sound. "And I still want that. Do you?"

I test my jaw to see if it works. Oh hey, it does. "Sure. That's why living together would be a bad idea."

"Absolutely. Besides, I'm sure I can get the money back from him."

My shoulders fall. "You already paid for the room?"

"First month's rent. It's not a big deal, and we'll clear it up. I'll get the money back."

The knife of guilt slices deeper. "Of course he'll give you the money back. Did you sign an agreement too?"

"Yes, but we're all adults here. If you want out, that's cool."

I take a drink of wine, noodling on his dilemma. If I'm kicking him out of a deal, I need to find a place for him. I need to understand, too, what he's looking for and why. "Why don't you have a place to stay?"

"I've been staying at my sister's house, as I said.

Her husband was called overseas shortly after the baby was born, and the timing worked out with me looking for a new job. I took one here so I could be near Jodie while he's in Afghanistan."

My heart lurches with sympathy. That's precisely what he told me when I pulled him over, minus the Afghanistan part. I can't imagine how hard that must be for his sister—and for his brother-in-law, to have to leave his family.

"How is she managing without him?"

"She's a tough cookie. It's not his first time having to go, so she's accustomed to it. But it's not easy, especially since she's a working mom."

"What does she do?"

"She's a baker. She sells the best walnut blue cheese bread at the farmers market."

Pride suffuses his voice as he talks about his sister. Hunger rumbles in my belly when he mentions the bread. "Jodie?"

His chocolate-brown eyes light up. "That's her. You know her?"

"I know of her. Her bread is legendary, and I might have been known to indulge in a loaf or two."

His smile spreads across his face. "That's awesome. I'll have to let her know. Seems like she's heard of you too."

This intel intrigues me. I take a drink of wine. "Is that so?"

His eyes travel along my body. "She might have mentioned yesterday that there was a pretty cop who worked at the market."

I might love Jodie even more, this baked goods goddess I hardly know. "Pretty cop? I'm flattered."

He takes another swallow, his eyes never looking away. "And I might have mentioned to her that I'd been pulled over by the prettiest cop in the entire universe."

Laughing, I roll my eyes. "And now you're just trying to butter me up to get me to let you stay."

"If I were trying to butter you up, I'd have brought some of the bread. Anyway, it's the God's honest truth. What can I say? I wanted you from the second you pulled me over."

Is there any word sexier than *want*? My skin tingles, and my bones hum from the boldness with which he owns his desire.

But this predicament isn't about desire.

It's about choices and circumstance, and, well, those pesky things known as bills. I sidestep his comment. "And it's not working out staying with her?"

"She's got three kids, and there are no extra rooms. I've been sleeping on the couch, so I'm looking for a place somewhere else to stay."

"It's tough to find rentals in this town," I say sympathetically. "The housing situation in California is insane, especially in wine country. It's hard for me as a regular person—news flash, I'm not making Mrs. Monopoly jack as a cop—to live here. The only reason I can is that my mom's aunt gave this place to Shaw and me when she passed away. She didn't have any kids of her own, and the mortgage is mostly paid.

I don't know what I'd have done without her generosity."

Derek nods then takes a drink. "It's settled, then. I'll set up a bonfire and make an offering to the rental gods that a generous aunt will come out of the woodwork and give me her cute little cottage."

"Derek," I say, a little sad.

He shakes his head. "Don't do that."

"Don't say your name?"

"Don't say it like that. With sympathy."

I lift my chin. "Hey. I'm badass. I don't have a sympathetic bone in my body."

"That's what I'm talking about. No sympathy, no mercy. I will find another place. It only took me a week or so to find this one, so I'm sure I'll unearth something else just as fantastic." His gaze wanders around my kitchen—it is definitely a cute home.

"How long was the agreement for?"

"We did a month-to-month."

I reach into the photo album in my mind, thinking of all the rental signs I've seen.

Hardly any.

Then again, I didn't post a sign. Rentals in this town are a landlord's prerogative. I get to pick and choose because I have what others want—real estate to lease. I honestly don't know of any other studios, apartments, or rooms over garages. "What is it you do for a living?"

"I'm a paramedic."

"Oh God," I say with a groan. "Couldn't you have

just said 'billionaire' so I could kick you out and not feel bad?"

"Sorry, kitten. I'm your regular blue-collar Joe. I've got some money saved, and a retirement plan, but for the most part, what you see is what you get."

What I see is damn attractive.

What I see is downright appealing.

I can feel the wine weaving its way through and softening me.

We're not that different. We're two adults trying to make a living helping people. We're not oozing money, but we want to serve the community. Taking a deep breath, I say, "Look, we can be adults, right?"

He scoffs. "What do you mean?"

"We're not animals."

He raises both brows in a question. "Speak for yourself."

"Well, if you were an animal, I'm sure you'd be a leopard."

"Jaguar," he says with a grin.

"Okay, jaguar. Hear me out. I'm not trapping you. You're not trapping me. We're both mature. We've already acknowledged we aren't looking to date or have a relationship, right?"

He nods emphatically. "Relationships are not on the radar."

"But doing our jobs is. I have a room above the garage that has a separate entrance. There's an entryway that leads upstairs, and the other door leads to the kitchen. I need to rent it to pay my bills. You need a place to stay in an expensive town.

You're here to help your sister and the community. I'm here to help the community. We'll be better at doing our jobs if we don't have to worry about paying bills or shitty couches that give us a crick in the neck."

He lifts a hand, absently stroking his neck. "How'd you know I have a crick in my neck?"

"I've never met a couch that's comfortable to sleep on."

He takes a drink of his wine, looking like he's considering this. When he sets it down, his eyes sparkle. "I hear there's a king-size bed in the room above the garage."

"Please. It's not just a king-size. It's a *memory foam* king-size."

He groans, and the sound is carnal and delicious. "Fuck, Perri. You're tempting me."

I laugh, take a drink, then focus again on the matter at hand. "I'm not suggesting we play house or have set times when you need to return home for dinner, or what have you. But I think we should rise above the fact that we're attracted to each other and solve this problem like grown-ups."

His eyes narrow, blazing darkly. He shakes his head.

"What? No?"

He sets down his wine, stalks toward me, and takes my glass. He puts it on the counter. He threads his hands around my neck, cupping the back of it. My blood runs neon-hot, and my body turns electric.

His face is inches away, and I can feel his breath

on me. I can smell the chardonnay, and the man, and oh God, I can tell he's aroused too.

He's barely touching me, but I can *feel* how hard he is.

My lady parts tingle, and I'm hot, wet, and wildly aroused.

"Let's get one thing straight," he growls. "What this is? It's not attraction. It's stronger. More intense. It's red-hot fucking desire. It's raw and it's carnal, and it's so much dirtier than attraction."

And I'm so much more turned on than I was a few seconds ago.

He lets go of me. I can't feel the ground. I reach behind me for the counter, needing to hold on.

"But we can't give in to it." My voice cracks as I try to speak around the fog of desire.

"I know that."

"We need ground rules," I insist. "Like, we share the kitchen, but you don't come down the hallway to my bedroom without permission. And I won't go up your stairwell without your permission."

His eyes darken with a dirty playfulness. "You can come up my stairwell anytime, kitten."

"I'm being serious."

"Me too."

"*Derek.*"

"Fine. You can come up the stairs, but no fucking."

"No fucking and no foreplay," I add, though I'm pretty sure the way he touched my neck was melt-my-undies-off foreplay.

"That leaves . . . kissing?" he asks.

A smile teases at my lips. "Well, we do need to practice."

"We absolutely need to practice."

"The contest is important for my potential promotion," I add.

"And I can't let you kiss anyone else."

"I don't want to kiss anyone else."

"I don't either." He grabs his wine and downs the rest of the glass. "So we'll live together, not fuck, not engage in foreplay, just kiss."

Too bad he just turned my legs to jelly with one seductive touch. But I do my best to keep my eyes on the prize. "Those are the rules. No mercy. No sympathy. We follow them, plain and simple."

I extend a hand to shake, and he takes mine in his, yanking me close, but not touching. I hear myself whimper, begging for him to cop a feel.

"We can do this. We can definitely make this work. Also, thank you." His tone is tender and earnest, and the gratitude in it tugs on my heart. "I've been dying at Jodie's home, and I can't wait to spread out and sleep on a proper mattress."

I smile, glad I can help. "And you will love it."

Our hands are still joined. We're still shaking and not letting go. He grips my hand tighter, his gaze straying to my lips. "But maybe we should enter the contest in the sweet category instead of the most passionate one."

"I can do sweet."

He drops my hand, cups my cheeks, tilts my head back, and dusts his soft, enticing lips across mine.

It's the polar opposite of yesterday's kiss. A soft, sweet whisper of a kiss. A chaste kiss. A kiss fit for a public square, a library, a dinner out. A kiss you can take home to mama.

But there's nothing chaste about my body's reaction.

Nothing sweet about the fire in my belly and the heat pulsing madly between my legs.

When he lets go, I blink, dazed. "Let me show you to your room."

He gestures toward the kitchen doorway, letting me walk ahead of him. I make my way to the staircase, and when I take the first step, he calls out, "Perri?"

"Yeah?"

"Are you a good witch or a bad witch?"

I turn around, cataloging the naughty glint in his eyes. "Guess you'll have to wait and see."

13

DEREK

I wake up feeling like Mark Zuckerberg.

At least, I bet that dude wakes up like the sun is shining for him.

Billionaires must feel fantastic in the morning, stretching their arms, enjoying their downy-ass pillows and fluffy-as-a-feather ten-thousand-thread-count sheets.

Or wait—do they sleep on greenbacks? Roll around on top of large bills all night?

Regardless, I'm sure they're comfortable at night, and I bet they feel rested as a hairy armadillo. My niece told me those little roly-polies sleep twenty hours a day, so they're another creature who are surely some well-rested mo-fos.

I wake feeling something else too. An early riser. No surprise, there's my clockwork morning wood.

But it's a brand-new day, because none of my sister's kids jump on me on the couch.

Halle-privacy-please-lujah.

With no worries about bumping into little ones, I swing my feet to the floor and walk straight to my own bathroom, my dick pointing the way.

I enjoy a long, hot shower and take care of business.

One thing remains the same though. My, ahem, inspiration.

Yup, I'm still using the same image. Red hair, pouty lips, tight body, and a uniform. There is something insanely sexy about a woman in a uniform. Man, I'd like to see Perri stroll through the door tonight all in blue, aviator shades on, cuffs at the ready.

For me to use on her.

She'd look spectacular shackled to my bedposts.

And there we go. Good morning to me.

By the time I'm out of the shower, I'm fresh and clean, ready to tackle the day.

I get dressed and head downstairs so I can say hello to my new housemate, but I find an empty kitchen.

My shoulders sag a little. I wave a hand, dismissing the thought that maybe I was looking forward to seeing her. I'll see her tonight.

I spot a chalkboard perched on the counter next to the fridge.

It's a cute little thing, resting on an easel, with an assortment of chalk in pastel shades resting on the ledge beneath it. She's written a note in lavender chalk.

Does she wear lavender lace lingerie too?

Hmm. Where is the laundry room? She did say she was washing her clothes last night.

Wait.

I'm not that big a pervert, or a Peeping Tom. I'm not going to check out her dirty—or clean—laundry.

Besides, a woman like her definitely wears sexy underthings.

I read her note.

There are eggs in the fridge. There's coffee in the coffeepot and bread on the counter. If you're gluten-free, you're shit out of luck. Otherwise, feel free to enjoy anything in the fridge. I'll see you later at the house, I suppose. Or not. :)

Well, that's as no mercy, no sympathy as you can get in a roomie. I nod, approving of her message. I like her style.

I whip up some eggs, make some toast, brew some coffee, and open the Stephen King novel I've been reading.

I'm not due at work for an hour, so when I'm done eating my breakfast in the company of a carny at a North Carolina amusement park in the '70s—*Joyland* is scary as fuck, and I love it—I grab my shades and the key that Perri gave me last night, and I walk the mile to my sister's house. Her kids are up, and it's a wild rumpus in the house. I give all the children smooches, ruffling hair and scooping them up in airplanes as they demand. I say hi to Jodie and tell her I'll take Molly to her summer camp.

Jodie's brown eyes dance with happiness as she gathers ingredients to bring to the industrial kitchen where she does her baking. "Stop. Just stop."

"You don't want me to take her?" I ask, surprised.

She makes a sound like a horse shaking her head, and Molly laughs from her spot at the table where she's drinking juice and drawing a tortoise.

"I do, I do, I do," Jodie says. "I just can't believe you're a literal angel."

I scoff. "Trust me, I'm no angel."

"Are you sure?" Jodie asks through narrowed eyes. "Because taking this little monkey to camp is saving my day."

"I can climb like a monkey. And I can talk like a monkey," Molly says, busting out her best monkey imitation.

I offer a hand to high-five my niece. "Molly Monkey, you deserve a banana."

The little blondie makes an agreeing sound, monkey-style.

I turn back to Jodie. "It's the least I can do. You have lots of baking on the agenda, and the bread isn't gonna make itself, is it?"

"I hope not. Self-making bread would put me out of business."

Molly tugs on my pants, hooting. "I'm an owl now, Uncle Derek."

I hoot back at her. "Yes, you are. I'm still waiting for you to master the peacock though."

"The peacock is hard to do," Molly says, frowning. "But I bet the face-painting lady can do it. She makes funny animal sounds."

My grin spreads of its own accord. I can't wait to hear the sounds she makes. When she's imitating ducks and cows and sheep, of course. "Does she now?"

My niece nods then points at me. "And she's better than you."

My jaw drops. "Take that back. Take that blasphemy back."

Jodie nudges me. "Guess you need to work on your animal sounds. Also, how is the new roomie?"

Last night when I stopped by to grab my bag, I told Jodie the basic details—I'd found a place a mile away and was moving. "She's the animal-sound lady."

Jodie arches a brow. "The pretty cop?"

I tap my nose. "Bingo."

She drops her voice to a whisper. "The one you spent a little time with at the market?"

Granted, she doesn't know the finer details, but I did let on that I might have hung out with the officer. "She's the one."

"And you're living with her now?"

"Indeed. I rented a room from her."

She yanks on my shirt and tugs me into the hallway. "*Derek.*"

"What?"

"You're renting a room from the woman you're

into?"

I bristle at her word choice. "I'm not *into her*. We were messing around. More like a Tinder thing." Though nothing about what I have with Perri feels like an online hookup. I know more about her from our brief encounters than someone I'd go home with from an app. I know she relies on her brother, she's close with her family, and she values her community. I know she cares deeply about her job, and also about the people in this town. She's sarcastic and sharp, and I've learned she's creative—with her mailbox and her curlicue chalk drawings.

Most of all, I know she has a strong sense of right and wrong, along with a soft heart and a fast mouth.

"And now you're living with her?"

"Renting a room," I correct, like the word choice is critical.

"Be careful."

"Why?"

Jodie taps my sternum. "The last time you lived with a woman she broke your heart."

I wave off her concerns. "Correction—the last time I was in a relationship, the woman turned out to be a lying, cheating you-know-what."

"And she broke your heart."

I wince, shaking my head. "Please."

"Derek," she says softly. "You had feelings for Katie. You cared about her."

"You are ruining my good mood. I'm over Katie. Completely over her."

"I know that. I'm saying it wasn't as simple as she

was *just* the woman you lived with. You were in love with her."

"Good thing I'm not in love with my housemate. And it's a good thing it's simply a mutually beneficial rental agreement to help out two fine citizens of Lucky Falls."

"Okay," she says, but her tone says she's not sure.

"I mean it. We're good."

"Just be careful. You like this woman, and you tend to fall faster than you think you do."

I scoff from here to Los Angeles. "As if that's going to happen." I shift gears like I'm spinning in a one-eighty on a racetrack. "I'm off."

I scoop up Molly, snag the keys to my sister's car, and take the little monkey to camp. When I return, I straighten up Jodie's kitchen, give the baby five million kisses, and tell my sister I'll see her later. I grab my helmet, hop on my bike, and head to work. Not even a crazy day where we're called to a vehicle crash on a winding road, then a swallowing incident involving a bet about marbles, can get me all the way down. It's like I'm a new man.

When my shift is over, I pop by the grocery store to pick up a few items, and head to my new digs, eager to see my housemate.

A small kernel of disappointment lodges in my chest when Perri's not home. I go to the gym, and when I return home later that night, the home is quiet.

I don't even run into her the next morning.

And that disappoints me more than it should.

But when I do see her again, her jaw drops.

14

PERRI

Elias bops.

His shoulders shake, his hips shimmy, and his head bobs as he leaves the police station a few feet ahead at the end of a shift, the evening after Derek moved in.

He hums some sort of hip-hop tune, then sings, "All night long . . . I want you all night long."

I call out to Elias, "Hey, Officer Jazzy Jeff. You auditioning for a talent show or something?"

Laughing, he turns around and waits for me as I head down the steps. "Something like that."

"Seriously?"

He motions for me to come closer. "You've seen those hot-cop videos, right?"

"Sure," I say tentatively. "I mean, it's not like I go online hunting for them, but I'm familiar with the concept. Like that one Gainesville PD did, right?"

"Yup." He waggles his hips, waiting for me to say

something. When I'm speechless, he fills the silence. "What do you think?"

As dry as a wine-country summer, I say, "I think you should keep your day job."

"C'mon, Keating. Admit it. I can groove."

I pat his shoulder. "Fine, you're a good dancer. But are you actually going to make a dancing video?"

He taps his nose. "Bingo. That's the plan. I'm hoping it'll impress the big man."

"A dancing video?"

"Well, if I can get it to go viral. Will you share it for me?"

"I'm not on Facebook. Besides, I think you want *others* to share it. People who have lots of friends and fans online. You want to get it in front of the right audience."

"Good point. I need to think this through more. Find some *influencers*, as they say."

His phone bleats and he grabs it, answering instantly. "Hey, honey bear." He mouths *the wife*, waves, and takes off.

As I walk to my car, awareness hits me square in the sternum. If he's trying to impress the big man, he's probably gunning for the promotion too. My jaw tightens. Reasonably, I figured I wasn't the only one who'd want the gig. Still, it's tough to go up against a buddy, even if the chief told me I should apply.

I weigh what I can do to increase my own chances for the role, but I feel a smidge guilty. Elias's wife is pregnant. Does that mean he deserves this more than I do? He has more at stake, doesn't he? I don't like the thought of competing against him, especially given his family expansion plans.

But that's life. Sometimes you have to compete against a friend, I tell myself as I stroll past the yarn shop. I pop inside to pick up another ball of merino wool and stop short when I see Jansen at the counter, his arms snaked around his wife and his lips planted on her cheek. I avert my gaze, but she calls out to me.

"Hey, crafty lady. I still have your yarn."

I look up and smile like I didn't just see them *practicing*. "Oh, thanks. Just need to get cracking on some new patterns."

She waves me over, and Jansen barks out a greeting. "Evening, Officer Keating."

"Evening, Chief."

"What are you making?" he asks.

His wife nudges him. "She's going to make you a new pink hat, Jeff. Now don't be so nosy."

I laugh. "It's okay. I don't mind sharing. I found an adorable sweater pattern, but I'm not sure who I'm going to make it for. But I find the routine of knitting helps me unwind."

"That's good. Personally, I like to do jigsaw puzzles," Jansen puts in. "That helps me let go of the unsolved mysteries at the end of the day. Like who broke into the jewelry store off Main Street the other month."

I frown. "I know. Me too. I wish we had more leads."

"So do I."

"Trust me, we all wish we knew what went on

there," Theresa says. The jewelry store theft is one of the few "high profile" crimes we've had to deal with recently in Lucky Falls.

"We'll get to the bottom of it. I'm confident of that," Jansen says, then fastens on a smile. "But I also want to know why so many damn people are speeding on Hollowstone Road."

That sparks an idea. Jansen did say the other day that he appreciated my willingness to do grunt work and pick up traffic duty without grumbling. "Want me to run traffic duty there this weekend?"

"That'd be great. Especially since some of them are likely to be DUIs. Let's get 'em off the road."

"I'll do it, sir," I say, deciding to ignore the dollop of guilt. I'm not taking anything away from Elias. I'm simply competing in the way that I have to. I'm doing my best to go above and beyond.

I take my yarn and head down the block to Helen's Diner, where I happen to know my trouble-making brother usually goes when he's done with work.

True to form, he's parked in his regular booth by the window, digging into his favorite roast beef sandwich. I rap hard on the glass.

He looks up, and I bug out my eyes and point at him. *You're in so much trouble*, I mouth, then head inside, march over to him, and push his shoulder. "What were you thinking?"

He stares at me, chewing slowly on the sourdough. "I was thinking how tasty this sandwich is."

"What on earth were you thinking, inviting that

man to rent my room? I'm going to wrestle you and take you down to the ground right now."

"Just sit and have a soda, Meryl Streep."

I sit across from him, staring. "I'm not being dramatic."

"Seriously, what is the problem? I thought we worked it all out."

"Listen, no joking, no teasing." I scan the joint for anyone in earshot, then whisper, "You know that guy is one hundred percent my type, and yet you asked him to live with me?"

"That's what you wanted me to do. Plus, you already made out with him." He shivers like the thought of me making out gives him the willies.

"Shaw, what have you known about me and men my whole life?"

"That . . . you haven't dated in a while?"

"Hello? Tattoos, ink, tall, dark, and handsome, bad boy. It's that simple. It's my temptation."

"You're not going to go to the bone zone, so what difference does it make?"

"You couldn't have found some nice, quiet, skinny accountant who drives a Subaru and spends nights with his calculator?"

Shaw cracks up. "You're never satisfied."

I slump down. "I appreciate you doing it, and Derek and I have sorted it out. But it's honestly one of the most insane things you've ever done."

"Some might say it's one of the most helpful."

"I'd have thought you knew better than to put me in that situation."

"And what situation did I put you in? Something where you can't handle your own hormones? You're a big girl. You're one hundred percent capable of keeping them in check."

The bell above the door rings, and Vanessa strides in. Shaw whips his head around, and I swear something changes in his dark eyes. Before she can reach us, I hiss, "Don't even think about it."

"About what?"

"Are you thinking of making a play for one of my best friends? You do know she is precious to me. And I don't want you and your ladies' man attitude anywhere near her."

He jerks his gaze back to me. "I've known her since she was six."

"And you will keep your playboy paws off her. She's like a sister to me. Which makes her like your sister."

He scoffs. "You do know she has her own sister? Also, I definitely don't think of Vanessa as *our* sister."

I don't even want to know how he thinks of her.

Vanessa reaches us. "Hey, guys. What's up?"

Shaw clears his throat. "We were just chatting about Perri's new roomie."

And I want to kick his shin all over again.

But I don't. Because I can keep my shin-kicking desires in check, right along with my hormones.

In fact, it's no big deal whatsoever.

Derek's not even home when I return that evening. I presume we're on opposite shifts, or he's out doing whatever he does when he's not home. Hell if I know what that is. But I do find a note on the chalkboard.

I replaced the eggs I ate. Have I mentioned I have a large appetite? Also, I picked up some of that coffee you seem to like. And I noticed you were low on Talenti Caribbean Coconut. Don't you know that's a crime, officer? You'll find some more in the freezer.

My stupid lips curve into an even stupider smile as I take out the pint and enjoy a few spoonfuls.

And I'm still smiling the next morning when I make my coffee.

* * *

Shaw was right.

I keep my hormones in check the next day, and not seeing Derek in the kitchen helps the cause immensely.

When I return home on Wednesday night, my hormonal state is as cool as a cucumber.

As I drive home.

As I park the car.

As I get out of the car.

And when I hear a voice. A sweet, bright four-year-old voice. "It's the animal-sound lady!"

But then I walk around the garage and stop in my

tracks. I run a hand through my hair, and my chest flutters.

Because holy shit. Derek is pushing a baby in a stroller down my walkway and holding the hand of the frog-loving little girl from the market.

Just like that, I zoom from cucumber-cool to red-hot chili pepper. These hormones are so very *not* in check.

15

PERRI

"Giraffe! Do a giraffe!"

The order comes from Molly, who introduced herself officially to me, along with the sleeping baby in the stroller. Today, Molly is tutu-free—she's decked out in cowgirl boots and a red cowgirl hat. I have no idea what sort of sound giraffes make, but the concentration distracts me from my libido.

I'm so damn grateful for giraffes right now, and for the obscurity of their vocalizations, forcing me to scroll through my mental list of animal sounds.

Perfect lust-killer.

I turn to Derek. "Any chance you know what a giraffe sounds like?"

He shrugs too, flashing a crooked grin. "I'm stumped. I bet Google knows."

Before I can grab my phone and ask the all-knowing search engine, Molly shakes her curly head and thrusts a piece of pink chalk at me. "I brought my sidewalk chalk. Can you draw a giraffe with me instead?"

"She's been drawing up and down the whole street," Derek adds.

I narrow my eyes and straighten my lips as I face Molly. "Aha! I see I've nabbed the mad Sidewalk Drawer. We've been looking all over for you." I stretch out my arms as if to grab her.

She squeals and clomps down the sidewalk in her boots, watching me the whole way and shouting, "Come get me."

I chase her, grab her waist, and declare "Gotcha" in my most over-the-top voice.

"Oh no! You caught me!" She giggles, and I let her go. "Now, draw!"

"Draw, please," Derek corrects as he pushes the stroller with the sleeping baby in it.

"Draw, please," Molly adds, batting her eyelashes at me.

"Now that you're in my custody, sure. I'll do it."

Molly laughs again. "Do it in blue. *Please.*"

"I will draw a blue giraffe. But would you let me change first?"

She sighs dramatically. "Okay. I'm not allowed to color in my school clothes either."

I smile broadly at her *we're all in this together* comment. "Exactly."

Derek stares at my work attire. "You don't need to change. You can draw in that, right?"

I toss him a flirty look, remembering his comments

from the other night. This man clearly has a thing for a woman in uniform.

All the more reason to change. Best to avoid temptation.

"Be right back." I head inside the house and turn the corner to my bedroom. I strip off my uniform and tug on exercise pants, a sports bra, and a tank top.

Then I go to the kitchen, pour a glass of water, and take a deep breath.

I can handle sidewalk chalk–drawing with a hottie pushing a baby and tending to his precocious four-year-old niece. After all, I don't even want to have kids.

Yet.

Maybe someday. But I definitely don't have baby fever, so there's no reason the sight of him with two absolute cuties should make my heart speed up or my skin sizzle.

I return to the front lawn, where the man looks me over again from stem to stern. "Nice yoga pants, but I still miss the uniform."

Spotting Molly twenty feet away, I whisper, "That's because you have some sort of uniform fetish."

He wiggles his eyebrows. "A big one."

"Why's that? You want to be cuffed? Told what to do?"

He scoffs and stalks closer, shaking his head. "Not at all, kitten."

The way he says *kitten*—so raspy, so commanding—sends a shiver over my flesh. "Not at all?"

"What I want is the complete opposite."

Holy hell, he can tell me what to do all night long. Tie me up, pin me down, cuff me.

Except I can't go there. *We* can't go there.

Fortunately, Molly skips to her Lou right on over to us, thrusting a bucket of sidewalk chalk at me. "You do a giraffe, and I'll do a hippo."

"Sounds like a deal."

And it sounds like what the doctor ordered to stop the quick spread of a lust relapse.

Molly squats on the stretch of sidewalk in front of my house.

"Giraffe time," I declare as I bend down to the concrete, working on the shape of the long neck as Molly draws a big bulbous blob for a hippo head. "That's not too bad."

She smiles. "I want to be a vet."

"For safari animals?"

"Yes."

"That's awesome," I say as I outline the tall creature's face. "So you'd be a big-game vet."

"Or I'll be a cowgirl."

"That could be fun too." I draw giraffe ears next, as Molly works on the hippo's belly.

"Or a ballerina, or a rock star."

"What if you're all four?" Derek chimes in as he joins us on the sidewalk. In the stroller, the baby's eyes flutter, and she stretches her little legs and arms, looking too adorable for words.

"Yes! I can be all four."

"You can be anything you set your mind to," I add as I finish the giraffe's tail.

"Whoa!" The praise comes from Derek as he surveys my handiwork. "You sure can draw."

"Thank you. It's just something I do for fun."

"That's a helluva talent for fun."

"Uncle Derek, you said a bad word," Molly calls out.

"Want me to arrest him?" I offer as I stand, dusting one hand against the other.

Derek offers me his wrists, his eyes twinkling. "Yes, please lock me up."

And I walked right into that one.

Devon's eyes flicker open, and I brace myself for a scream, but Derek swivels around, scoops her up, and peppers kisses on her cheeks.

And, I'm a ghost pepper. I'm the hottest jalapeño in history. Wait, nope. I'm the surface of Mercury because of the way Devon coos and tugs on his beard.

That's it. I'm a goner.

"She sure likes you," I say as casually as I can while he nuzzles the cutie-pie.

"The feeling is quite mutual."

"How old? Six months?"

"She's six months and two days," Molly interjects as she scoots down the sidewalk to work on the hippo's tail. "Come join me."

I make my way to Molly. "You do his face," she tells me.

I swivel around and fill in the hippo's eyes. "And how old are you?"

"I'm four years, eleven months, and sixteen days."

"Wow. You sure are a very specific counter."

Derek bounces Devon on his hip. "Molly also loves to talk. Shh. Don't tell anyone."

"Uncle Derek!" Molly chides.

I smile. "That's cool. I like to listen."

Molly chatters on about her favorite animals, her favorite friends, her favorite clothes, and her favorite games as we illustrate an entire savannah in front of my home while Derek holds the baby and plays with her.

It's weirdly . . . domestic.

It's also thoroughly unexpected.

I didn't anticipate coming home and finding my hot housemate playing with his nieces.

"Where's your nephew? Doesn't your sister have three kids?"

"He's playing basketball," Molly answers.

"At a friend's house," Derek adds, and Devon cuts him off with a wail.

"And someone is officially hungry." He glances at the time on his watch. It's past six thirty. "We should go. Make you guys some dinner."

Molly claps. "Can we have dinosaur nuggets and french fries?"

Derek shakes his head. "No, you can have chicken and broccoli."

Molly's nose wrinkles, making it clear what she thinks of that idea. "Pretty please."

He shakes his head. "If you don't like that, you're welcome to have a delicious salad of beets, carrots, and organic apples."

"Gross." Molly makes a gagging sound.

"C'mon, then, porcupine. Time to go." He glances at the artwork, then turns to me, his eyes landing on mine. "Guess I'll see you later, officer."

A strange feeling envelops me—the wish that he'll say, "Let's have a drink," or "Want to watch a show?" or "Should we grab a bite?"

But those are crazy thoughts, so I shake them off.

My stomach doesn't though.

It rumbles loudly.

"Someone wants chicken and broccoli," Derek teases.

"Seems I do," I admit.

"I'll make you something later if you'd like." The offer is sweet and completely welcome.

I smile and say yes.

As I head inside, I feel a little buzzed, a little tipsy.

A little like my feet don't touch the ground.

I've seen a whole new side to Derek, one I never imagined existed when I met his flirty, cocky, handsome ass on the bike. Just a few days ago, he was a typical bad boy, dirty to the bone. But I've learned he's determined, straightforward, and giving too.

He cares deeply for his family, and he dotes on his nieces. He's devoted to his sister.

And we share a passion for work with the community. We both wake up every day and help others. Being a cop—and being a paramedic, I presume—can be thankless, emotionally draining, and woefully underpaid work.

And yet, I wouldn't change it.

It's not my hormones banging the drum inside my body as I go into my house.

It's some other part of me. A part I haven't exercised in a long time. A part I don't let out to play very often.

That dumb heart.

Even though I told my brother I have a type, the problem is, that type doesn't usually work out in the end. I've dated, and I've had some semi-serious boyfriends, but the last person I liked—*really* liked—was Nick, who ran a tattoo shop in Santa Cruz. I'd met the growly, inked artist on the boardwalk one weekend when I was there for a girls' getaway.

Nick and I hit it off in the way that two people who don't live in the same place can. Our connection was instant and electric. He was 100 percent my type, and I was utterly gaga over him.

So gaga, I managed the three-hour drive to Santa Cruz as often as I could, visiting him on weekends and whenever I had time off, this little arrangement going on for several months.

He was sexy and funny and hot as sin.

Turned out he had a girlfriend too. Just hadn't mentioned her to me. Slipped his mind.

Oops.

I was the other woman.

Since then, I've been as cautious as I can, dating locally, screening men online through and through.

What the hell? Why am I thinking about dating? Derek and I aren't dating. We aren't an item. He just offered to make me dinner.

I head to the gym to work out and work off these silly hormones.

Yes, they're just hormones.

That's all.

When I return, I don't see him. I take a shower, loop my wet hair in a ponytail, and tug on shorts and a tank top. I dust on some powder and add a pinch of lip gloss, then head to the living room where I turn on some music.

It's eight thirty, and I'm ready to eat the table.

What the hell?

This girl has had a long, hard day, and she's hangry.

That's when I hear a key clicking in the back lock —the door that leads directly to the room above the garage. Will he go straight upstairs or come downstairs to the kitchen? And why do I care? Why do I even want to see him? I like living alone.

I flip through my sweater patterns, and when his footsteps fade, telling me he went upstairs, I grit my teeth and try to tamp down my disappointment. I shouldn't be disappointed. In fact, I'm not disappointed at all.

I study my patterns, trying to decide what to make and who to make it for, when I hear water running.

The shower.

He's taking a shower.

He's naked in my house.

What the hell was I thinking?

What the hell was *Shaw* thinking?

I head to the kitchen, pop a frozen pad thai meal

into the microwave, and grab it before it's fully cooked. I take the dish, a napkin, and a fork to my room and shut the door.

Sitting on my bed, I shovel the half-warmed pad thai into my mouth, then I grab my laptop and open up the reports I've been working on. *Work.* That's what I'll do. Work on reports to impress the chief.

I don't think about Elias. I don't entertain the dash of guilt. And I definitely don't think about my roomie who ditched me.

It's not like we had a date.

Not really.

Well, maybe it felt a little bit like one.

And that's just the problem.

16
DEREK

The next day, Hunter slams the door of the ambulance, getting in after our third ER visit, then breathes a sigh of relief.

Scrubbing a hand over his jaw, he says, "For a while there, I thought we were about to be anointed the new angels of death."

"It can feel that way some days."

It's been a rough morning so far. We came close to losing our first patient en route to the hospital after a heart attack, then our second when a woman had a severe allergic reaction to a bee sting, and came even closer with this call—a scary-as-shit workplace accident. The guy lost a ton of blood after falling off a ladder, but we made it through the ER doors in time. He's in the capable hands of the doctors and nurses now, and all we can do is hope for the best.

My stomach rumbles. "And it's lunchtime."

Hunter pats his belly and cocks his head as if

listening to his stomach too. "Yup. Mine says it's time for In-N-Out Burger."

"Dude, you can't live off burgers and fries."

"Like hell I can't. I'm going to get me two double-double burgers today."

During my first week on the job, my partner has plowed through an astonishing amount of fast food, devouring enough fried chicken, wings, and burgers dripping with fixings that I feel in danger of a second-hand coronary. "Are you trying out for one of those all-you-can-eat contests?" I ask as he puts the van in reverse to pull out of the hospital parking lot.

Hunter waggles his eyebrows as he steers. "Hey, that's a damn fine idea. I can put down more hot dogs than you can dream of."

"I assure you, I do not dream of hot dogs."

"But I like this food contest plan. Maybe I can meet a nice new lady at a hot-dog-eating contest."

"Do those type of contests have ladies in them?"

Hunter flips the blinker as we head toward the street. "I don't know, but I imagine a woman who can scarf down hot dogs is my kind of lady."

I groan. "I haven't eaten yet, and you're already ruining my lunch."

He laughs as he heads to the nearest In-N-Out Burger. I love that place, but I can't survive on it every day, so I pop into the grocery store next to it, grab a chicken salad, and meet Hunter outside.

He eyes my meal suspiciously. "Are you a vegetarian?"

"One, you say that like it's a bad thing. Two,

there's meat here in this salad." I point. "Right there on top of the lettuce is a food known as . . . wait for it . . . chicken."

He lifts his supersize soda and takes a thirsty gulp. "But where's the bread, man? No way can you survive on greens and meat."

I shield my eyes from the bright noon sun. "Have you never heard of Paleo eating, man?"

"Eating dinosaurs? More power to you—I bet those things have tough skin."

"I assure you, I'm not eating velociraptors. But if I were, I'd opt for a skinless, boneless breast." I spear another piece of chicken. "I do eat bread, but not too often. I'm all about fewer carbs and more veggies and protein."

Hunter digs into his double-double burger and gives me a knowing nod. "Ah, I get it now," he says around a mouthful. "You're probably a tree hugger too. I bet you're even a pacifist."

I chew, then answer. "I like trees. I like veggies. I like protein. I like peace. So sue me."

He cracks up after he finishes his bite. "Just giving you a hard time, man. I dig trees too, and peace is cool. But I am also a burger and bread man, and nothing is going to change that."

I shrug with a smile. "I say potato."

"I do not say po-tah-to," he says indignantly, making the second syllable rhyme with *ha*. He grabs a french fry. "But I definitely say 'french fry.' I also say you can indulge in a fry now and then, Mr. I-Have-a-Twelve-Pack," he says, mocking me.

I pretend to check out my abs. "Yup. Definitely a dozen lady-killing abs working overtime underneath this here shirt."

We laugh and joke as we finish our lunches.

This is good. It feels like I can settle into this town with guys like Hunter. I don't know where I'll wind up long-term, or if I'll ever stay in one spot. But for now, with my sister and the rug rats and the guys from work, Lucky Falls feels doable.

Except for the little issue of living with Perri.

That's not a long-term solution. Living with a chick you want to bang is more complicated than I'd thought.

Or maybe it's just that living with a woman at all is complex. They're like those math riddles on standardized tests—if a train leaves at noon, and there are ten passengers, which one is Mr. Red? And the answer is five, or who the fuck knows.

I figured she'd get a kick out of yesterday's new chalkboard note, but nope. She didn't even respond to it this morning.

That afternoon, we're called to what Hunter tells me is a regular's home.

"Mrs. Jones has emphysema. We take her in a couple times a year. She's a sweet old bird, but she still smokes."

I shake my head. "Wish that shit didn't even exist."

"We can agree on that for sure."

After we take her to the hospital, Hunter tells me he needs to make a quick phone call, and that he'll meet me at the van.

As I exit the hospital, I spot a police cruiser pulling up, and the possibility that it might be Perri has me more excited than I care to admit.

The driver cuts the engine and steps out, and, oh yeah, there she is.

Looking edible.

I wait outside, enjoying the view of her walking toward me. The way her uniform fits her gets my blood going. Maybe she'll respond to my note now. Her face is impassive, though, and her eyes are obscured by her aviators.

"Hey, officer." I wink. "Fancy meeting you here."

She lifts an eyebrow. "It *is* the hospital. I'm here from time to time."

"And what brings you in today?"

"I need to take some additional statements for my report on the three-car accident," she says.

"I don't think I was called to that one. Any serious injuries?"

"Broken arm only, but there are some issues I need to dig into."

"Good luck with the issues."

"Indeed."

Indeed? What the hell? Are we operating on an *indeed* level now? I step aside, and she strides by, nodding. "Gotta go."

Then she turns and heads through the sliding doors.

I scratch my head, get into the van, and wait for Hunter. When he slides into the driver's seat, I say, "Women, right?"

Hunter nods, even without any context. "Women."

Some days, that's all you can say.

Women are just too hard to figure out.

Especially when they give no flirty replies to your clever chalkboard messages.

* * *

As I get ready to clock out, the boss man strides over to me and parks a hand on my shoulder. "Good work on your second week," Granger says. "It's almost like you've done this before."

I smile, since he knows I've put in a decade. "Yeah, just a little bit."

Granger's expression turns more serious. "Hoping you like it here. We need regulars. We need guys to stick around."

"Sure," I answer. What else can I say? My situation hasn't changed since lunch. But this job and this town work for now.

Granger squeezes my shoulder. "Let me know if I can do anything to help you settle in."

I'm tempted to ask if he knows any long-term places to stay, but I need to handle this Perri awkwardness first. I won't run without reasoning it out—or trying, at least.

"Thanks. I will."

I leave, heading to the gym for a workout, where

Hunter texts me that the guy with the heart attack is doing better and the ladder fellow is stable.

I smile as I reply between sets.

Derek: And you are not an angel of death today.

Hunter: There's always tomorrow, mwah ha ha. And now I must go consume a pizza.

Derek: I'll cheer you on in the pizza-eating contest.

Hunter: Go eat a leaf, bro.

I close the thread and resume my workout, listening to my audiobook as I lift harder and heavier, the sweat dripping down my chest, my muscles burning. When I'm done, I head to the lot where I keep my bike. Briefly, I think of my sister, and how straightforward she is. If Perri's irked at me for Lord knows what, the least I can do is be up front.

I text her to give her a heads-up on when I'll be home, figuring it's the least I can do if she's got an issue with me.

Derek: Be home around 7:30.

Perri: 10-4

I stare at the reply like if I look hard enough, I can decipher it. Decode the hidden meaning.

But what the fuck? TEN-FOUR?

Ten fucking four?

Jesus Christ. What did I do to her?

Along the way to my bike, I pass A New Chapter, and I duck into the local shop to grab some goodies for the rug rats. In the kids' section, I find a picture book on safari animals, then an early reader on basketball and baseball for Travis. I grab both and head to fiction to see if there's a copy of *Mr. Mercedes*. I left that book behind in the move and keep meaning to reread it.

I'm hunting through the shelves when a blonde woman strides by, smiles, and asks if I need any help. I tell her the name of the book.

"We just got a new paperback shipment in. Let me grab it."

"Thanks so much," I say, instead of ten-four. Because, hello? Who the hell says ten-four?

Except, well, maybe cops and rescue workers, I admit to myself grudgingly.

I head to the counter to wait for the blonde lady, and a furry calico rubs up against my leg.

"Hey there, sweet pea," I say to the kitty, and she proceeds to rub her face against my leg, kicking the purr box into high gear. "Well, meow to you too." I bend to scratch her chin, and she offers a most appreciative *meow*. "You're one pretty lady, aren't you?"

The cat rubs harder, purrs louder.

"It seems Clare wants to adopt you," the blonde says as she returns to the front with a book in hand.

"She's a sweetheart, and I'd take her up on it if I could."

The woman laughs. "You should hear what my boyfriend says about her. Gabe is convinced Clare is plotting his doom."

I laugh. "Your man has jealousy issues with the cat?"

"Something like that," she says, then her eyes linger for a second on my arms. "You're Derek, aren't you?"

"I am. How'd you know?"

"Shaw mentioned something at dinner the other night. We're all friends. I'm Arden."

"Nice to meet you, Arden. And if you know Shaw, you must know Perri, then."

Arden smiles warmly as she scans the book. "I've known her since we were six. She's one of my best friends."

"Yeah?" I want to ask a ton of questions, but I'm not sure where I'd start. Except I'm damn curious what the hell makes that woman tick. "Hope she said nice things about me."

Arden simply smiles, her eyes roaming over my arms again to the sunbursts and arrows on my skin.

That makes me think that Perri did indeed say nice things about me. I have a hunch I know exactly what she told her friends.

And that reminds me that I do know what makes Perri tick—a helluva lot.

She told me so herself.

I'm going to have some fun with Miss Ten-Four.

Oh yes, I am.

17

DEREK

Her car is outside, so I know she's home. But I don't look for her. That's not our deal. I head to the back door, unlock it, and peer down the hall. I don't see her in the kitchen.

That's fine, especially since my first order of business is a shower.

It's almost always a shower. After the gym, after work, whatever. I need the time to wash away the day and let it go. Too much goes on in my life, too many things I can take home with me. It's best to find a way to shed them.

For me, that's a hot shower.

After I dry off, I grab a pair of basketball shorts and tug them on, then hunt for a T-shirt. I snag a gray one from my duffel and pull it over my head, then I stop.

I know this woman's weakness.

And I'm going to exploit it.

Because I fucking can.

Tossing the shirt to the bed, I make sure the waistband of my shorts rides low, and I go downstairs. When I open the door to the kitchen, I call out playfully, "Honey, I'm home."

I swear I can hear her roll her eyes.

"Hey." Her voice is emotionless.

"Can I come into the witch's den?"

"Lair. It's a lair."

"May I enter?"

"At your own risk."

I walk into the kitchen first and see my note is still up on the board. What the hell? How could she not like this note? It's fucking adorable, and I am not an adorable man. Huffing, I grab the chalkboard and carry it to the living room where she's curled up on the couch in yoga clothes, her hair in a ponytail, her knees up, and her head bent over her laptop. I brandish the chalkboard in front of my chest. Let her wait before she can see the twelve-pack I'm packing. "You working?"

She doesn't look up. "Yup. Reports. Trying to work on this jewelry store—" She glances up, narrowing her eyes. "What are you doing?"

"Did you not see my awesome note?"

She licks her lips. "I saw it this evening when I grabbed an apple."

I eye her suspiciously. "You. You, who are addicted to coffee? You're telling me you weren't in the kitchen this morning?"

She shakes her head. "No, Detective McBride. I

was not at the scene of the chalkboard crime. I had to leave quickly. I grabbed coffee at the station. I didn't even go into the kitchen."

"But you saw it tonight?"

"Yes, I saw it a little while ago when I returned home, and I'm also seeing it now, since you're shoving it in my face."

My gaze drifts down to the words I wrote in pastel yellow chalk. "Read it to me."

She sighs, as if thoroughly annoyed. "Why do you want me to read it to you?"

"Because you've been giving me the cold shoulder, Miss Ten-Four."

"My text reply was warranted. You'd only sent me a heads-up message."

I tap the chalkboard. "And this is not a heads-up message. This is fucking flirty. Read it aloud."

A smile tugs at her lips, and she seems to fight to rein it in. She draws a breath and reads. "*Sorry I didn't make it back in time to whip up a delicious chicken and broccoli dish for you. I'll make it up to you. I promise. Also, I know what sound giraffes make. Ask me. :)*"

I stab a finger against the board. "I used an emoticon. I hate emoticons."

She smirks. "Okay, what sound do giraffes make?"

"I'm not telling you till you say you're sorry."

She laughs. "For what?"

"For assuming I was a dick."

"I did not assume you were a dick," she says, challenging me.

"A little dick?"

She gives me a sassy look. "Oh, I don't think it's little."

I laugh. "It's not little at all. It's exactly the size you want."

"Is it?"

"Kitten, you know you want to ride me."

She rolls her eyes. "That is not what we're talking about."

"We're talking about how you thought I ditched you."

"I didn't think that," she says, defensively. Too defensively.

"You did. You thought I stood you up and didn't leave a note, and you gave me the cold shoulder at the hospital, and then the cold text."

"I had to take a report on a three-car crash! My colleague who's up for the same promotion had just walked in ahead of me. We were working."

Fine. She makes a fair point. But still, it's time to pull out all the stops. I drop the chalkboard, and she gasps.

It worked.

I walk closer to her, half-naked, giving her the full view of my chest, abs, and V-line. Maybe I'm cocky, maybe I'm overly confident, but I don't give a shit. I've worked my ass off to look good shirtless. Pretty sure Perri likes what she sees a lot, judging from the way those green eyes eat up my chest, stroll over my abs, and linger on my hips, where a flock of silhouetted birds flies up the V-line and around my hip.

"You . . ." she says, like there's sand in her throat.

"Me what?"

She points at my birds. "Your . . ." It's like she's having heatstroke.

"You okay? Need CPR? I can help."

"No," she says, swallowing roughly.

"You see something you like, then?"

She shakes her head, but she doesn't stop staring at my abs. I put my hands on the arm of the couch and lean in. "Now, admit it."

"Admit what?"

"You were annoyed that I was home late, because you wanted to see me."

She scoffs. "I just wanted your food."

Defiant creature. "Nope. I don't buy it."

She lifts her chin. "I like chicken and broccoli."

"And you want me to cook for you, don't you?"

"Of course I do. One less thing I have to do myself."

"Then admit you wanted to see me."

Her voice softens to an embarrassed whisper. "No. Yes. Derek, it's stupid, okay?"

"So you did?"

She shrugs, her eyes vulnerable, her smile guilty. "Fine. I was having a fun evening with you and your nieces, and I thought dinner would be nice, and then you weren't here, and I was hungry, and it's dumb to get annoyed because we're just housemates, and it's fine."

Her sincerity hooks into me, reminding me that I did break a promise. "I really am sorry I didn't make it back in time to cook you dinner like I said. I left the note when I came downstairs, but you were already in your room," I say softly.

"I went to bed early."

"And I had to shower because the baby spit up all over me."

"Oh no. Is she okay?"

I wave a hand. "Babies will do that."

"You're really good with her."

"I adore that little chunk of love."

Perri smiles. "I can tell." She takes a deep breath. "Anyway, it was silly. I wanted to have dinner last night, and that was a stupid thing to wish for. Then I rushed out this morning, so I didn't see your note, and when I saw you at the hospital, I was trying to be all business-like since Elias was there, and plus, I *should* be business-like. When I came home, I *did* see your note, and it was sweet, and it made me feel stupid for having been annoyed at all. I was annoyed with myself."

"And then you saw my ink."

She shoots me a saucy look. "More like you thrust your abs in my face."

I give her a dirty grin. "Pretty sure you liked it."

"What makes you think that?"

"The way your eyes went all glossy and hazy. The way you're staring shamelessly at me. The way your nipples are poking through your shirt."

Her jaw drops, and she looks down at her chest then crosses her arms. "My nipples are not hard."

"Must just be an optical illusion," I say offhand.

"Exactly. Also, back to more important matters. What sound do giraffes make?"

I stand up, move around the couch, and sit next to her. "They hum."

"Giraffes hum?"

"They do. And that's the sound you're going to make when I kiss you again right now."

I grab her hair and devour her delicious lips.

18

DEREK

Maybe she doesn't sound exactly like a giraffe.

More like a pent-up, turned-on woman who wants what I have to give her. It's a kiss to drive her wild. A kiss she can take to bed tonight, that she'll bring under the covers, replaying every touch and taste so she can get herself all the way off in mere minutes.

That's how I kiss her.

Like I want to fuck her. That's the only way this woman ought to be kissed. Her back is against the couch cushion, and I lean into her and crush her lips, claiming her with my mouth. With my hands. With my body.

I bring her closer, letting her know that when I kiss her, she's all mine.

She moans into my mouth as I grapple with her ponytail, yanking it down, letting the lush strands fall over my fingers.

As I do, she murmurs, sinking into the kiss, letting

me guide her head back to expose that seductive neck. A neck I've wanted to touch from the second I met her.

As I kiss her senseless, she melts under me. I tug harder on her hair, and she moans louder. Her head falls against the pillow, and I let go of her lips, traveling to the V of her shirt.

She whimpers as I kiss the hollow of her throat.

"You like that?" I flick my tongue over her skin, and she nods, panting a hot, breathy *yes*.

I give her more of what she likes, mapping her neck with my mouth, kissing the column of her throat, making her squirm with every touch of my tongue and brush of my lips. Her hands inch up my chest, her fingers playing over my abs, my pecs, the waistband of my shorts.

But I know this woman's needs. I grab her hands, thread my fingers through hers, and pin her wrists at her sides. The sound she makes is one of bliss as I grip her like that, kissing her neck, her ears, her hair, until she bows her body up off the couch.

"You're so turned on," I murmur.

"It's your fault."

"I'll take all the blame."

Then I grip her hands tighter, and in a flash, I shift positions, sinking to half recline on the couch and pulling her on top so she straddles me, knees on either side of my thighs.

"We can't do this." Her green eyes are wide with hunger and questions. "Remember? No mercy, no sympathy?"

I let go of her hands and run my fingers up her neck and into her red locks. I tug her hair. "I'm not breaking any rules."

She grinds her pelvis against my erection, and a shudder racks my body. She dips deeper, rubbing against my hard shaft, creating a delicious friction even with my shorts and her yoga pants between us. Lust rolls around inside me, flooding every corner. "Feels like you are," she whispers.

"Is it a crime to be turned on in the presence of a beautiful woman?" I jerk her against the outline of my cock, moving her hips so she rubs and drives me out of my fucking mind. Pleasure grips me in a white-hot blur of agonizing desire.

"No crime here," she pants as she rocks against my erection. Her eyes float closed and her shoulders sink, and she grinds. Dipping, rising, swiveling . . . It's the most erotic thing I've ever seen, and somehow it's even more erotic as I watch her face, cataloging her expression as it shifts from deepening pleasure to wild need to exquisite torture.

"Fuck, kitten. You're going to look so good riding my cock."

She nods slowly as if she's in a haze. Grabbing her wrists, I move them behind her back and grasp them tighter. She breathes harder, letting me know she likes it when I take control.

"Yeah, just like that, kitten. Keep doing that. Keep rubbing against my dick. Get yourself off."

"I don't think . . ."

"You don't think what?"

Her lips part. Her lids are heavy. "I don't think there are kisses like this in the contest."

"Fuck the contest. Fuck me instead."

She opens her eyes, and I've never seen a woman more on the brink. "We said . . . we wouldn't . . . do this."

"Do it once. I won't tell you broke the 'no foreplay' rule. Ride me till you come hard."

She sinks against my hard-on again, grinding herself on me, rubbing harder.

Then she squeezes her eyes shut and pauses midgrind. She counts to three aloud and snaps open her eyes.

She's a different woman now. Cool, calm, in control. How the hell does she do that? She's like the clap-on-clap-off device.

"Can we rewind? Go back to the chicken and broccoli?" she asks, calm as a yogi.

"Seriously?"

"This is too dangerous when we're living under the same roof."

I groan, releasing her wrists. My head drops, falling to her chest.

Oops.

Bad idea.

I'm in her tits.

Wait. Nope. Good idea, great idea, best idea ever. I'll just curl up and spend the night in the valley between these two perfect globes. Except there's something I want to know. "How did you go from nearly riding me to kingdom come to wanting broccoli?"

She pats my head, threading her fingers through my hair. "I'm a hard-working woman, and I'm hungry."

I raise my face. "You can work hard on my dick."

She laughs. "Where's that restraint, McBride? Where's that whole let's-follow-the-ground-rules attitude?"

I cup her cheeks hard, loving the way her eyes fill with flames in an instant. "That was your idea, kitten."

"You went along with it. We agreed." She lifts an eyebrow. "Plus, to answer your question, I have excellent restraint."

"Oh, is that so?"

She smiles proudly. "I do. It's impressive, my resistance."

"What a cocky babe you are."

"Takes one to know one."

I laugh then groan in frustration. Because my brain and my heart know she's right. I can't let the overwhelming lust I feel for this woman carry me away. I'm living with her. I desperately need a place to stay. And fucking would absolutely fuck it up.

So I can't *screw resistance*.

I collect myself, gently move her off me, and affect a good-boy smile. "Look, I'm not even aroused anymore."

That's a lie. I'm sporting huge wood.

Her eyes drift to my lap. "Yup. Not even aroused in the least. Nor am I."

I roam my eyes over her. Flushed cheeks. Swollen

lips. Beaded nipples. "Good. Because you don't seem turned on at all."

"I'm so not turned on. I totally wasn't about to orgasm."

I shrug nonchalantly. "I definitely wasn't on the cusp of coming in my shorts like a teenager."

She laughs, letting her head fall into her hands as she cracks up.

When the laughter subsides, she stands, her hair messed up, her cheeks rosy. "Listen, we need to behave. We both want and need the same thing. We need each other as roomies, not as lovers. Besides, neither one of us wants anything more."

"Exactly. Screw relationships. Let's have some grub."

And on that cock-blocked note, I head into the kitchen and cook for my woman.

I mean, my landlord.

The hot, sexy landlord who nearly came on my lap.

19

PERRI

I do have excellent resistance.

Well, most of the time.

I'm not winning any medals in restraint tonight, but I'm disciplined in general and always have been. In college, at the academy, at work now—I get in, do the work, go the distance.

But there's always temptation to lose focus, and Derek McBride is the strongest temptation I've ever known. But temptation doesn't pay the bills. That's why I used the trick I learned ages ago to yank myself out of nightmares—count loudly to three and wake myself up. Making out with Derek, and riding his hot, hard ridge, was a flirty, dirty dream rather than a nightmare, but the same trick worked.

One, two, three.

And I was out of the zone.

Now here I am, in the kitchen, watching him cook. The sight of him making my dinner is testing me, and I'd like to snake my hands around those abs, explore his twelve-pack, and trace all his ink.

Must resist . . .

One, two, three.

There. Better.

But still, there's just something about a man who can make a meal.

Double points if that meal is for me.

And triple points if he surprises me, which he's doing. He's not just throwing together the basics. He's whipping up a chicken stir-fry, adding in asparagus, carrots, and peppers then tossing in spices, and my mouth is watering.

"You might be the perfect roommate," I say as I pour myself a glass of wine and offer him a beer.

He arches a brow as he sautés the chicken. "How do we have beer? Pretty sure I forgot to pick some up when I was at the store. I bet I was undressing you in my head in that aisle, and that's how it happened. Slipped my mind when I slipped off your shirt."

Laughing, I grab a bottle of pale ale. "I snagged some myself. I had a feeling you were a beer man. Was I right?"

He looks over at me, a smile edging his lips. "You picked up beer for me?"

"Why, yes, I am the perfect housemate. Go ahead and say it."

He winks. "Perfect landlord. And yes, I'm a beer man. But I'm an everything man, truth be told. Tonight, though, I'll take a beer gladly."

I uncap it for him, and he accepts, tipping the neck

against my wineglass. "To your resistance. May we see how long it lasts."

I clink my glass. "It'll last *so* long."

He shakes his head, smiling as he turns down the burner.

A few minutes later, he's served the stir-fry.

I grab the plates. "Want to eat standing up?"

He scoffs. "Kitten, I made you a meal. Sit your ass down at the table."

"Well, la-di-da." I shake my ass as I move to the table.

"Yes, do that. Do more of that, and I won't feel bad at all at my resistance cracking in two."

I shake my butt once more before I sit.

"Temptress," he mutters as he digs into his food.

I take a bite of the meal, and it's delicious. "You can cook."

He wiggles his brows. "I can indeed."

"What other hidden talents do you have?"

"I'm quite handy."

"Me too," I say, grabbing another forkful.

"That so?"

"Can you imagine an un-handy cop? Lame."

"True that. What are you handy with?"

"I can fix a washer. Hang a door. Change a tire."

He wipes a hand across his forehead. "You need to stop being so hot."

I lift my wineglass and enjoy another sip. "You have a thing for competent women?"

He wiggles his eyebrows. "Competence is so sexy." I smile at that.

We eat some more, and I ask him to tell me about his sister. "What's Jodie like, besides being an amazing baker? Were you always close?"

"We were. She's five years older, so she's been like a second mom my entire life. Her dolls became useless once I arrived. She doted on me instead."

I smile at the sweetness in his tone when he talks about her. "That's adorable."

"I remember at one point when I was in middle school, my parents were talking about some changes in the dress code at school and Jodie said, 'And what is Derek going to wear? Are you going to let him wear gym shorts to school? Because I don't think it's a good idea.' And my dad said, 'Well, we won't have to worry because Derek has a third parent in you.'"

I laugh. "That's sweet and funny."

He takes a drink of his beer. "She's always looked out for me, so I figure the least I can do is the same."

"And your parents? They're not around?" I ask carefully.

He shakes his head. "Died a few years ago. It's just us." But he doesn't sound sad, more like he's accustomed to this reality.

"Sorry to hear that."

"Me too, but they were older, and it was their time, I suppose."

I nod, understanding him. "I hear you. It's still sad, but when you can make peace with a loss by knowing that—well, that's a good thing."

"It is." He takes another bite, chews, then adds,

"Anyway, that's probably another reason why Jodie and I are still close."

"Did she ask you to move here when her husband was assigned overseas?"

"I volunteered. My contract was up in San Francisco and I'd heard about the gig, so it seemed like a good time. Plus, I was getting tired of the insanity in the city. I don't mind the change."

"Is her husband in battle?"

He shakes his head. "Nope. He's a military chaplain."

My ears perk. "Oh, that's interesting. You don't hear about that often."

"He's a minister a few towns over. He had this chance, and Jodie wanted him to take it. He really wanted to help the troops."

My heart squeezes for his family, for the guts and bravery it takes to help others who put themselves on the front lines. "That's lovely, and lovely, too, that you came up here to help."

"It's nothing anyone else wouldn't do." He shrugs. "What about you? I take it you're close to Shaw, even though it seemed like you wanted to wallop him the other day."

I laugh. "That about sums us up. We needle each other pretty much all the time. I think it's because we're eleven months apart. We've always competed for everything."

"Everything?"

I finish my last bite and set down my fork. "Yup. We were in the same grade at school too."

He smiles. "No kidding."

I hold up a hand to vow. "It's the truth. I was the youngest, and he was the oldest, and I was kind of crazy motivated, but he was too. We competed for everything—affection, praise, sports, grades, who did chores faster. It created this bizarre dynamic. Still does."

"But it works for you guys?"

"Weirdly, yes. I love him madly, but he exasperates me, and I know he loves me, even if we want to kill each other sometimes."

We finish dinner and as we wash our plates, Derek mentions Arden. "I met your friend at the bookstore earlier. She said she's known you since you were six."

I smile widely. "She's like family to me. So is Vanessa. We're all so close."

"She seems like she looks out for you. And I had the distinct impression you told her about me," he says with a sly note as I set the last plate in the dish rack and turn off the faucet.

I wipe my hands on a towel. "And what gave you that impression?"

He shrugs in that way that cocky men do—casual, sexy, confident. "The way she checked out my ink. Almost as if she was *told* about it by a certain . . . *kitten.*"

I snap the towel against his waist. He grabs it and tugs me close. "It's okay that you like my tattoos. You can touch them too."

Like that, he lights the match, and the fire in me roars through the roof. I'm a flame around him.

Maybe right now, I'm not so flame-resistant. I run my eager fingers up his strong, muscular arms, then down them too, tracing the sunbursts and bands, loving their look, savoring his skin.

He murmurs, a husky, raspy sound that heats my blood, that makes a pulse beat between my legs.

"There's more to touch, Perri."

"I know," I whisper, dancing my fingers down to his birds, tracing the outline of one, then another, traveling perilously close to the waistband of his shorts, and what lies beneath. What I desperately want more of.

He breathes out hard, rough. For a second, maybe more, it hits me—I have this power over him. He wants me in the kind of bone-deep way I want him. Sure, he's told me from day one, but his body says, undeniably, how much he craves me.

Resistance, I remember.

I need it.

There's so much at stake. The job. The rent, since I haven't had a reliable tenant in ages. My goals, because I want that promotion. I've worked my butt off for it. I need to keep my eyes on the prize.

I dust a quick kiss against his delicious lips. "No mercy, no sympathy."

"Damn your mantra."

"*Our* mantra," I correct.

He steps away, his dark eyes holding my gaze. "Kitten, I'd like to find out how strong your resistance is. And I fully intend to test it."

"How will you do that?"

"You want to win your kissing contest, right?"

"I do."

"Then we will be practicing every night. And you'll be practicing your resistance. Mark my words."

With that, he turns, heads to the stairwell, then up and out of sight.

It takes every ounce of my resistance not to follow him up the steps.

20

PERRI

The next morning, I find a note on the chalkboard.

What about air kisses? That's a category for sure. We could own that one.

I laugh, grab a piece of chalk, and write under it.

No doubt you'll find a way to practice them.

I snatch a peach and head to the backyard. After taking a bite of the fruit, I fill a pitcher from the spigot and water the plants on my deck, musing on air kisses as I feed the thirsty fern, the grateful tomato plant, and the ravenous blueberry bush.

"All better now?" I say to the plants.

They sigh contentedly, I imagine. I sigh happily too, chewing a bite of the peach as I wonder how exactly we'd own the air kiss category. We'd ace it . . . that's the trouble.

I head inside, toss the peach pit in the compost bin, erase my first note, and write a new one.

After all, we're in the midst of a new competition. A who-can-hold-out one. With a pastel blue piece of chalk, I write a new response in curlicue letters.

I can absolutely resist your air kisses. Just try me.

Dusting off my hands, I snag a spoon and grab a yogurt from the fridge. I dive in, feeling a little zip from my snappier retort. I pop in my earbuds as I eat at the counter—standing up, thank you very much—and I toggle over to the morning news, catching up on the latest in local politics, then check on press releases from nearby agencies before I switch to the scanner to see if there's anything going down that I need to know about.

I catch myself tensing, as I often do when I switch, braced for bad news. That's, well, the reality of my job. But it's relatively quiet, so I relax my shoulders with a sigh of relief. I finish my breakfast, then brush my teeth, dress in my uniform, and head to my car. As I hit the unlock button on the key fob, I hear the heavy thump of shoes.

I spin around. Derek's mere feet away from me, in his blue work pants and a T-shirt with the number of his EMS unit on it, looking like he's ready to perform CPR or bandage a wound. Because he is.

He mimes tipping his hat to me. "Morning, officer."

"Morning, troublemaker."

"You think I'm a troublemaker?" He scrubs a hand across the scruff on his face. *That scruff.* That lucky scruff.

I'm scruff-resistant though. I lift my chin and cross my arms. "I know you're a troublemaker."

His dark eyes twinkle with mischief, and his grin hints at exactly the kind of trouble he likes to make. "Is that so?" He comes closer, then closer still, until he's inches away. His chest is dangerously near my arms. His lips are in my zone. My breath catches, and my senses do the salsa because he smells clean and freshly showered, and I sure do love that scent. I don't think he wears cologne—it wouldn't make sense for his job. But his unadorned scent works for my libido, because I love the natural soapy smell. I love it so much, I think I'm humming.

"Mmm."

He gives a devilish grin. The *most* devilish grin. Then he quirks an eyebrow and leans in, dusting a kiss a centimeter, no, a millimeter, wait—a fraction of a millimeter from my cheek.

My hum turns into a traitorous moan.

He pulls back, his dark eyes full of naughty deeds.

I lean against the metal of the car and swallow, catching my breath.

He brushes the backs of his fingers along my jaw, and against my will, against my better judgment, I lean into the stroke of his hand, like a cat.

"You're right," he whispers. "You are excellent at resisting air kissing. Need to up my game."

He winks and turns around.

One, two, three.

I recover speech. "You were toying with me?"

He glances back. "Of course, kitten. You threw down the gauntlet last night. And you should have expected nothing less."

He strides out of the garage, heads to his bike in the driveway, and mounts it. Tugging the helmet on, he gives me one last knowing look, then peels away.

I'm still standing at my car, stupidly turned on from an air kiss on a Friday morning.

* * *

At work, Elias shows me his smoldering gaze.

Then he displays his bump and grind.

After that, he says he wants to demo what he calls the hippity-hop.

I raise my hand like I'm in school. "What on earth is a hippity-hop?"

"Picture me riding a pogo stick."

"Do I have to?"

"Oh, c'mon. My viral video is going to be big."

I'm at my desk tackling paperwork before I hit the streets. I wasn't planning to be a dance judge.

But I sigh. "Fine. Do it."

He jumps up and down as Jansen strolls by. "Nicholson, I hope you never defile my eyes again with that move."

Elias's face sinks. "Seriously, Chief? You don't think I have game?"

"I'll think you'll have game when you do this." Chief stops, shimmies his hips, then adds in a snap of his finger.

Holy smokes. My boss can dance. "Chief, you need to be in the video with Nicholson."

Jansen smiles and winks. "If you're doing a viral video, you need to have the right moves."

I laugh, look at Elias, and point to the boss. "Evidently, he knows what they are."

Jansen claps Elias on the shoulder and shows him a few dance moves, and I smile at first, but then a new emotion digs into me. *Worry.* Is Elias a better contender for the job? Is this dance video going to seal the deal for him? More importantly, am I a fool for thinking a kissing contest has any bearing on a promotion?

I answer the question for myself. The contest is simply a fun thing to do, a bet with friends, and a chance to raise money for rescue workers.

I'm not going to win the promotion with a kiss. Puh-lease.

I'm a cop, not a performer.

I'm going to win it with work. Good old-fashioned, nose-to-the-grindstone work. I reroute my focus to the daily grind, making sure all my reports are spit-shined and polished, then spend a few extra minutes reviewing the jewelry store case.

Something nags at my brain, a potential suspect we didn't consider seriously, and I mention it to the chief later in the day.

He scrubs a hand across his jaw. "That's a possibility, Keating. That's a damn fine thought. Keep looking into it."

"I will, sir."

I ignore the fact that he's humming Elias's hip-hop tune as I leave his office.

* * *

"And that's how you have happy abs!" The declaration comes from the Pilates instructor, who's vicious and cruel the next afternoon. In a nutshell, she's everything I want a Pilates instructor to be.

"Thanks, Millie," Vanessa says, and I add my thanks too.

My core barks at me, spewing invectives as I head out of the studio. "Nothing like Saturday traffic duty followed by Pilates," I say.

"Sounds like a perfect day. Did you nab any speeders?"

"Lots of them over on Hollowstone. Just like the chief wanted me to do."

"Such a good girl. I'm dying to hear all about how

fast they went above the speed limit, but why don't you tell me first, since you've been so damn busy all week . . . how's your fabulous new housemate working out?" Vanessa inquires as we reach the sidewalk. She stares at me with wide eyes as if to say *spill the beans*.

I smile. "He's a multi-purpose roomie. He made me dinner the other night."

She wiggles her eyebrows. "So he knows the way to your heart?"

"Ha. It's merely the way to my stomach, and my stomach is grateful."

"Aside from his culinary skills, do you like having temptation right under your nose?"

I furrow my brow. "What makes you think I'm tempted?"

Vanessa chuckles, clutching her belly. "Oh, that's cute. That's super adorable the way you said that. Especially with that line between your eyebrows as if you hadn't a clue what I meant." She taps my forehead for emphasis.

I toss her a look. "How did I say it?"

"Like you actually believed it."

"I do believe it."

"Perri, you can't fool me. I know you're tempted. Just be honest. How hard is it?"

I smirk, thinking of precisely how hard Derek is. I toss her a knowing glance. "As hard as it needs to be."

Her jaw drops, and she smacks my elbow. "Tell me everything, you minx."

The memory of the other night washes over me. The way I straddled him on the couch. The filthy things he said. The hard, hot length of him. "There's not much to tell. We made out, but we stopped. Because I have damn good resistance."

"That doesn't entirely sound like the definition of good resistance. That sounds like the start of something deliciously dirty."

"Hello? Hot man in my face, and I'm mere minutes away from a mind-blowing O and I *stopped*? That's hella awesome. I've always had good resistance. And I will keep having it with him."

"What makes you think you have stellar resistance? I'm just curious."

We turn the corner toward the town square. "For one, I never drank or did drugs in high school or college. I had no problem resisting that."

"True, but isn't Derek more tempting than drugs? You were never into drugs or alcohol."

"Exactly. So I'll be fine."

"But you've always liked tall, dark, and inked men. Do I need to remind you of Nick?"

I hiss. "No, please don't. He was the biggest ass of all the asses."

"How about Cody? The guy you dated after college. He had bad idea written all over him." Evidently, Vanessa is taking me on a tour of the ghosts of boyfriends past. Tonight's edition stars the handyman who worked in one of the nearby vineyards when I was in my early twenties. We fell into a fast and breathless relationship. He'd come over late at night, keep me up after hours, and ask me to skip work and play.

"And I had discipline resisting his bad ideas. Remember? I broke up with him the second he asked me to start paying his bills."

"You're excellent at knowing when to get out of a bad relationship. But sometimes you're drawn to them."

"But Derek's not a bad man," I point out quickly.

Vanessa whips her head around, and we stop in front of the olive store. She stares at me like she's caught me sampling an olive without using a toothpick. "So you do like him."

Her eyes are like a magnifying glass seeing through me. I'm not entirely sure I'm ready to be seen, so I let the light shine on a portion of the truth. "Obviously I'm attracted to him. We're doing the kissing contest."

She tilts her head and gives me *the look*. "It's more than attraction, Perri. You like him. And it's not about the contest. If you truly wanted to, you could enter the friendly kiss category with a friend. Derek's different. You like-like him."

"Are you giving me the double-barrel 'like'?"

She smirks. "I sure am. Guilty, officer?"

I take a deep breath, wanting to deny it, wishing I could. But I do like him. He's so much more interesting than I thought. He's so much more than a simple flirty, dirty biker. He has layers I never expected, a good heart, a great soul, and a kindness that reaches deep down inside him. He's that rare breed of man who ticks every box on the checklist.

Except one.

He's not interested in a relationship. He told me point-blank that day in the waffle truck.

Relationships aren't my thing these days, he'd said.

That makes two of us, I'd replied.

He said it again when we established the rules of living together.

Relationships are not on the radar.

A strange heaviness settles over my heart, but I dismiss it quickly. Relationships aren't on my radar either. That's why it's pointless to worry and to wonder—neither one of us is interested in entanglements.

"I do like him, but it doesn't matter since I don't want any entanglements, nor does he."

"Really?"

"Yes, really. We're both on the same page. We don't want more."

"That's what we say until we do want more," Vanessa says, softly and wisely. Too wisely perhaps.

"But right now, I don't. Plus, I've got my eyes on the prize," I say, waving my hand behind me at the station, thinking briefly of Elias and his efforts to land the promotion. For a second, I want to tell Vanessa how it makes me feel, but I'm also all feeling-ed out right now.

I point to the olive shop. "Now, olives—those I can't resist." I grab her arm and head into the shop. "It's your turn. Have you picked a fabulous cause for your part of our bet?"

Vanessa nods excitedly. "Wine and bowling!"

"Is bowling better with wine?"

"Everything is better with wine. I'm teaming up

with one of the vineyards for my bowling competition fundraiser. A little wine-tasting along with going for strikes. All the funds will be used to help local animal shelters with the fire rescue relief."

"Damn. Now I want you to win."

She smiles. "But really, we all win."

"That might be the cheesiest thing you've ever said. But also the sweetest," I say, then I buy some olives and head home, curious if Derek will be there when I arrive. I didn't see him last night because our work schedules clashed, but perhaps tonight will be different.

But even if I don't see him, I'll be fine. I don't want more.

I say it again to drive the point home.

21

PERRI

I pull up to my house. Has he left me a note today? If there's one inside, will it make my stomach flip?

I look in the rearview mirror. "Settle down, lady cakes. You don't need a note. You don't need a man. You don't need a thing."

When I'm inside, I avoid the kitchen. I head to my bedroom to shower and change. After considering yoga pants again, I opt for a summery skirt instead, adding a tank top to keep it casual. Perusing the outfit in the mirror, I decide I've pulled it off. When I check the time, I've successfully distracted myself for five minutes.

I head to the kitchen, looking for a love letter.

I mean, hunting for something easy to make to eat.

The first thing I see isn't food.

It's a note, and it gives me goose bumps.

This is your fair warning, not that you deserve it. But I plan to test your resistance shortly.
With another type of kiss.

I close my eyes, wishing, hoping. The hope dashes through me, warring with my resolve. When I open my eyes, Derek's here, in the kitchen, wearing next to nothing.

"How do you do that?"

"Do what?"

"Walk around like a cat. I didn't hear you."

He points to his feet. "It's called no shoes."

"Still, you're so quiet. You're like a Tesla."

"I'll take that as a compliment."

I stare at him, wishing I didn't like the view so much. Attraction is so annoying. He wears basketball shorts and nothing else. My temperature rises, along with my frustration. "I thought we agreed it made no sense for anything more to happen."

"What makes you think something is going to happen?"

"Because you're . . ." I flap my hand at him.

"Shirtless?"

"Yes. You're so shirtless, and so ripped, and it's so not fair."

He laughs. "I didn't realize you were so tempted."

"You're tempting, and you know it."

"Want me to put a shirt on?"

"Yes. No. Whatever."

"Excellent. That's what I was looking for."

"To mess with my head?"

His eyes stroll up and down my body. "Your fantastic head, your lush mouth, your sexy-as-sin body. The whole package, kitten."

"Why do you want to mess with me?"

"I just want to practice." He takes my hand and places a soft, tender kiss on the top of it. That kiss has the audacity to send shivers through me.

"Hand kissing?" I tremble.

"It's an old-fashioned art, don't you think?"

"Yes," I say, trying to keep a stony face. But there's nothing old-fashioned about my response. My lady parts are dancing the hula and they want a luau with him.

"How was your day?"

I blink at his one-eighty. Are we *how was your day* people? "Are you really asking how my day was?"

He smiles as he reaches into the fridge, grabbing bread, fresh slices of turkey, and tomatoes. "I'm really asking. Mine was delightful, by the way. I spent it with the rug rats while Jodie prepped for the market tomorrow. Took them to the Charles Schulz Museum. Molly loved it. That dude could draw."

I love that place, and I'm tickled that Molly did too.

"Isn't it amazing how he could bring Snoopy and Charlie Brown to life with just line drawings? That museum is cooler than you'd expect."

He brings the sandwich stuff to the counter and finds the cutting board. "Right? I never thought about how adding Franklin would be a big deal in the sixties. A teacher suggested it in a letter."

"I love the collection of letters from readers. There's something about a handwritten note that feels like the writer is putting more of their heart onto the page."

"Or on the chalkboard," Derek says, glancing at the message board. "But I digress. How's everything with you?"

I lean against the counter and tell him what went down at work the last few days, catching him up on the latest with the possible promotion. "And Elias is up for the promotion too," I finish, sharing with him what I didn't tell Vanessa earlier. Maybe I need a guy's perspective. "It's hard going up against a friend, especially since his wife is pregnant."

He looks up from the cutting board with a frown. "What does that have to do with it?"

"I feel guilty. Like he deserves it more since he's going to have a family soon."

Derek points a finger at me, his expression turning tough, no-nonsense. "Are you good at what you do?"

I square my shoulders. "Hell yeah."

"Then don't fall into that trap."

"What trap?"

"The trap that single people fall into. We get asked to do more overtime, stay later, come in on holidays because we aren't married and don't have kids."

"True," I agree, thinking of times when that burden has fallen on me. "And I went in today to do traffic duty, but that was a choice. I volunteered."

"Exactly. You made the choice. You volunteered. You weren't roped into it." He slaps some turkey slices onto the bread.

"And I've been digging into this jewelry store theft case that's been bugging the chief. I haven't cracked it yet, but I *chose* to take on the work."

"Good. We have to remember our time is as valuable as anyone's. There's this weird societal notion that only parents and married people deserve a break. But every human does. And everyone deserves a chance to go after what he or she wants. You've earned it. So don't feel one damn ounce of guilt."

I hadn't been looking for a pep talk, but I'm grateful he gave me one. "Thank you. I needed that."

He offers a fist for knocking. "We relationship-free people need to look out for each other."

There it is again—the reminder. Not that I need it. I'm a card-carrying member of that club. So I keep it on the same level, asking about his work. "How are things with your job? Do you like your partner?"

He tells me about Hunter and Hunter's belly, and before I know it, he's entertained me and also whipped me up a yummy-looking sandwich. I take a bite and declare it delicious. He grabs it from me and takes a bite too.

I wag a finger. "Hey, you're stealing my food."

"Damn straight I am."

"Fine, you can share."

"That's what I thought."

We trade the sandwich back and forth till it's gone. "Want another?"

I act indignant. "Of course, since you ate half of mine."

"Every now and then I can't resist bread." He makes another sandwich, and we share it again.

"You like the guys you work with? Do you consider them friends?" I ask.

He nods, but it's the half-committed kind. "Sure."

"You should do something with them. Go out with Shaw and Gabe. Hunter too. Get a drink."

He taps my nose and purses his lips. "Aww, you're trying to get me to make new friends. You're sweet."

I roll my eyes. "I'm not sweet."

"You're so sweet, Perri. Admit it."

"I'm not sweet."

"You are. You want to play friend matchmaker."

I huff. "And to think I was going to invite you out with the group."

He grabs my arm. "Yes. I'll go."

"Invitation rescinded."

"No, it's not. You invited me, and you meant it." He tugs me closer. "Didn't you?"

I swallow as my skin heats from his nearness. *"Derek."*

"What?"

"You're tempting me," I admit.

He drags me against him all the way, letting me feel the full length of him. "You tempt me."

He's so hard, so aroused, and I am too. Heat pools between my legs, and I ache for him. "Why are you doing this?"

His hand snakes around my waist, across my hips

to my ass. He cups one cheek, and I nearly go up in flames. When he squeezes, I whimper. I want him so much. I want him to grab me, lift me up on the counter, and strip me to nothing.

To take me.

"Because . . ." he whispers, then brushes his nose against mine. "Because I want this to be so hard for you."

"You're evil," I whisper.

He squeezes harder, his cock steel against me. "I'm the worst."

"You're killing me."

"I'm dead too, if it's any consolation." Gently, he brushes a kiss to my forehead. "Forehead kiss. Want to enter in that category?"

I tremble. This man. He's breaking down my resistance in too many ways. "I don't want a forehead kiss."

He lets go of my butt and tucks a strand of hair over my ear. "I don't either." Turning around, he puts the sandwich ingredients away and points to the stairwell.

"On that note, I'll be upstairs with nothing on. Resist that." He shoots me a cocky grin, his eyebrows rising.

He turns and walks away.

The fucker.

He walks away.

I want to yell.

I want to stomp my feet.

Mostly, I want to go upstairs and find him.

Naked, aroused, imagining me.

Dragging a hand through my hair, I exhale deeply and formulate a plan.

Then I smile. It might even be an evil grin. The next morning, I leave a note on the chalkboard, and head to work with an even eviler grin on my face.

It's payback time.

22

DEREK

For the record, I'm not one of those guys who's into chick flicks.

I'm your standard-issue, horror-loving, thrill-seeking guy. I don't need war flicks or blow-'em-up movies, but I do dig the scary stuff more than anything else.

And way more than kissy-face movies.

When Katie used to make me watch them, I always talked during the kisses. Because the kisses were boring. C'mon. They aren't real, and they're hardly sexy. One night during her five hundredth rewatch of *You've Got Mail*, I asked her what we were doing that weekend right as Meg Ryan said, "*I wanted it to be you*," and I received the kind of dirty look that men spend a lifetime trying to avoid.

But when I find Perri's note telling me to get ready for a movie kiss reenactment this evening, I don't think I'll be bored.

Now showing: At 9 p.m. tonight, please come to the theater of the living room prepared to reenact a movie kiss. Remember—practice makes perfect.

Yep, I'm not foreseeing boredom. I'll be wildly aroused. Insanely turned on. And loving the flicks in a whole new way.

At the farmers market, I help Jodie at her booth, though I do manage to stroll past the face-painting one a few times, and I wink at Perri. The guy next to her makes a poodle balloon for a girl, and I half want to sneer at him. For no other reason than I know he's the one going after her job.

Hers.

That promotion belongs to Perri. She's fierce and tough and devoted. She works hard after hours. She's a go-getter. She should get the job.

I return to Jodie's booth then spend the afternoon with the kiddos, but most of the time, I'm thinking about practice.

That evening, I find Perri on the couch at the appointed time, waiting for me, iPad in hand.

I lift an eyebrow. "You're not going to force me to watch those movies, are you?"

She rises, and my eyes nearly pop out of my head. She's wearing . . . a tiny sports bra and shorts so short they're nearly underwear.

My brain short-circuits, and my body goes haywire.

She's too sexy for my own good.

She's curvy in all the right places and trim in all the other ones. Toned and tight, with tits I need in my mouth.

"I'm not going to force you to do anything." Her voice is smoky.

I clear my throat, trying to wrestle some control over the situation, but I'm pretty sure I have none as she walks toward me, impossibly sexy and with just enough gloss on her pouty lips to make me want to kiss it all off.

She leans against the arm of the couch, crosses those toned legs, and tells me to join her. I move next to her, my skin sizzling at how damn close we are and how much closer I want to be. She swipes her finger on the screen and taps on a clip of the best movie kisses of all time.

"We can try reenacting *Gone with the Wind*, *Ten Things I Hate About You*, and even *Spiderman*, which would be tough to pull off but could totally win us the contest on account of how hard it is to do an upside-down kiss in the rain. Or we could do *Dirty Dancing*, when Baby crawls across the floor to Johnny."

"Sure," I say, my voice gravelly because I don't care which one we do. I want them all. I want her.

She shows me the reel, and it's a blur because I'm thinking of her body and the way she smells and how she looks. Soon enough, she shuts the cover of the iPad and tells me to sit on the floor like Swayze did in

Dirty Dancing. She turns around, gives me the naughtiest look over her shoulder, then walks a few feet away. She swivels back, drops down to her knees, and proceeds to crawl to me.

Across the floor.

This is the best roomie situation ever. She's the perfect housemate. Yeah, come sit on my face. Come ride me.

She reaches me, meets my lips, and kisses me so softly and sweetly, it blows my mind. My dick would like to be blown too, and he's announcing his desires loud and proud.

Perri slinks closer, deepening the kiss. She swipes her tongue against mine and ratchets this moment to a whole other level. She's fierce and fiery, and she kisses me with an intensity that makes my cock swell and my desire shoot through the roof.

I want to take her right now. Have her right here. Fuck her on the floor, on the couch, anywhere, everywhere.

She's insistent and in control, even on all fours, kissing me. She rises to her knees, and my desire shoots to the sky. *Touch me now*, I want to growl, and maybe my wish is going to come true, since her hands are on a fast track for my crotch.

But they land on my thighs.

And you know what? That feels pretty fucking good too. She presses her palms hard on my legs, inching close to my cock as she kisses me.

"The other night," she whispers, breaking the kiss.

"Yeah?"

"After the forehead kiss. When you went upstairs and you had nothing on . . ."

"What about it?"

"Did you get yourself off?"

I groan. "Damn straight I did."

She murmurs. "You, in bed, jacking off. *Hot.*"

"You can come help me tonight," I rasp, shuddering as lust surges through me. As I picture her finding me, joining me, wrapping her hand around my dick.

I'm burning up with a wild longing for her. I grab her wrists, drag her even closer. Her eyes drift down to my hard-on, tenting my shorts.

She licks her lips. "Will you be jerking this perfect dick in your bed in a little while?"

Holy hell, she is the vixen of my dreams with her filthy little mouth. "I'd much rather you do it for me."

Her lips curve up. "I bet you would."

"You want to, kitten?" Fuck resistance. Fuck ground rules. I need to fuck her.

"I'd love to . . ."

I'm ready to pull her up, toss her over my shoulder, and carry her upstairs. "Now. Let's go now."

She smiles like that's all she wants in the world. Then the smile transforms. Naughtier, more mischievous. She lets go of me, sighs contentedly, stands, and brushes her hands down her thighs. "That was great practice."

What the hell? Is she high? Is she tripping on something? Because there's no way she said that.

I rub a finger against my ear. "That was practice?"

She blows me a kiss. "Of course. Just like the times you teased me. No mercy, remember?"

I burn with frustration. I'm amped up to the moon. I'm a lethal combination of aroused to the ends of the Earth and annoyed to the center of it. I point at her. "Don't forget the no sympathy part. That means you, woman. You want to play this game? Then you are on."

She lifts her defiant chin. Nibbles on the corner of her lip. Arches an eyebrow. "Bring it." She winks, sways her hips, and saunters down the hall. When she reaches her door, she turns around, slides her hand down her chest on a fast track to her waist, then lower. She teases her fingertips against the waistband of her shorts.

My dick tries to chase after her, the rest of me army-crawling behind it if need be.

"By the way, I'll be in my room, naked and thinking of you as I replay that." She dips her finger inside her waistband before she spins around.

A second later, her door clicks shut.

Payback isn't a bitch. Payback is a hard-as-stone dick that's desperate for attention and not getting it.

Screw silver-screen imitation.

Forget my own attempts at air smooches, old-fashioned lip-locks, and any other kind of kiss.

It's time to throw out the playbook.

That's what I intend to do, before I detonate from lust.

23

DEREK

I've applied pressure on wounds. I've felt pressure to pay bills. But I'm learning a whole new meaning of the word as I imagine Perri while I ride to work, as I picture her between calls, as I see images of her lush body flash before my eyes no matter what I do.

During a break, I hit up Merriam-Webster to make sure I'm clear on it. There are a handful of definitions for "pressure": "the action of a force against an opposing force," "the stress or urgency of matters demanding attention," and "a sensation aroused by moderate compression of a body part or surface."

That all sounds about right. But there's one missing—*the stress of wanting your roommate naked, under you, calling your name . . . but too bad, sucker, because you're engaged in a war of resistance with her.*

Yeah, this pressure is a fresh category of dick affliction. Doctors will soon determine it's worse than blue balls. It's the albatross of horny men everywhere.

The pressure spreads to my lungs, making me think of her with every goddamn breath. It expands to my brain, where every bit of gray matter is stuffed with thoughts of her.

Her face, her body, her mouth. All I want is to touch her, have her, taste her.

Even work doesn't distract me. The gym doesn't erase her from my mind. A shower certainly doesn't do the trick.

And an evening blowing bubbles for Molly and the baby and shooting hoops with happy-go-lucky Travis does zilch to move the implacable space she's commandeered in my head.

The pressure only intensifies.

When I leave Jodie's and return to the house I share with the woman I crave like oxygen, like water, like food—well, that was a dumbass decision living with her, wasn't it?—I'm finished playing games.

Because the doctors say there are two treatments for this disorder.

One is ending the flirtation.

The other is ending the flirtation.

Maybe I started the kissing games, but I'm going to finish them tonight.

When I walk through the back door, I call her name.

No answer.

Dragging a hand through my hair, I huff, ready to blow a gasket. I'm a geyser. I'm a fire hydrant. Something has to give.

I head to the kitchen, grab the chalkboard, and

write a note, scratching so hard I nearly leave gouges in the blackboard. I step back and stare at the seething letters. Even my handwriting looks charged.

I stomp upstairs, grab my book, and dive into a story of a small town upended by a violent crime and disturbing supernatural forces. The escape from my reality only minimally calms me.

After nine, I hear the lock click. A key slide. A door open.

My heart rate speeds up. I close the book.

Dressed in jeans, a T-shirt, and my bare feet, I go downstairs. As she drops her purse to the counter, she flicks on only one light, so the kitchen is barely illuminated. The light-blue dress she wears is elegant and sexy at the same time.

It accentuates every curve of her body, every inch of her figure that I want to explore. But she could wear a grocery store bag, and I'd still want her. This desire for her is more than physical. It's burrowed deep, much deeper than how she looks. I wanted her the moment I met her, and the more I've come to know her, the more profound the longing has become.

"Were you with Arden and Vanessa?" I ask.

She startles then turns around. "Yes. How did you know?"

"You're dressed for women."

Her lips curve up. "I am."

I walk to her, saying her name in a rough voice, ending the small talk. "*Perri.*"

The moonlight casts half her face in a silvery glow. "What is it, Derek?"

"Read the note."

She peers at the chalkboard.

Practice is over.

She looks back at me, a new vulnerability in her green eyes. Maybe even concern. "It is?"

I cross my arms so I'm not tempted to touch her. There will be no coaxing hands or whispering lips. This is about choice—choosing what we do next. No more games.

"I'm going to be direct here."

"Okay. Be direct." Her tone gives nothing away.

I nod at the board. "We're done practicing."

"I can see."

"The game has changed."

"Has it?"

The time for bluffing has passed. "All my cards are on the table. This is how it's going to be. The way I see it, this flirtation needs to end."

She squares her shoulders, lifting her chin. "Fine." She says it like the tough girl she is.

"It can end one of two ways."

"Is that so?"

"It can end cold turkey."

She winces but nods. "Fine."

"Or it can end the other way."

"What's that?"

"Let me lay it out." I point to her hallway—her do-not-go-down-it hallway. "You can go to your off-limits room and do what you did last night. You can slide your fingers inside your panties and get yourself off." Her eyes widen like I've nailed it. "You can pretend it's me licking you or sliding inside you or whatever you imagine. And you can come that way tonight."

A breath rushes from her lips. She licks them, raises her chin, and whispers, "And the alternative?"

I let my gaze linger on her face, then I take my time perusing the rest of her. Hard nipples, quickened breath, eyes darkened with desire.

"The other option is this." I gesture to the steps. "I go upstairs, and you follow me a minute later."

"And what happens upstairs?" She's so damn direct it arouses me further. Because it suggests she's done with the games too.

"Up there, the games are over. No more resistance —no more toying. We give in to this." I gesture from her to me. "We give in to what's been happening from the second you pulled me over. I haven't once stopped wanting you. I want you more every day. You're under my skin and in my head, and right now, I need to fuck you. And you need to fuck me."

Her breath hitches. "Is that what I need?"

"Only you know. But you sure look like you want to get on my cock and ride me."

She gasps.

I step closer. "And that's where I want you. But you also look like you might need me to put you on your hands and knees and slide into you, fucking you so damn hard you scream."

"That's what you'd do?" She's breathless, and her hand flutters over her chest.

I give myself another up-and-down tour of her body. "Or you might look like you want me to spread your legs and devour your sweet little pussy with my mouth and tongue."

"Those are a lot of options you've just laid out," she says, a little flirty, a lot dirty.

I grin. "Consider it lady's choice tonight. You come upstairs, and you can take your pick from the No More Practice menu. I'll be waiting."

She hums, and it hits an octave I've never heard till tonight. "Is that what happens in the room above the garage?"

I lift a hand and finger a strand of her hair. She trembles as I touch her. "Come find out."

24

PERRI

There are hard decisions. There are easy decisions. And there are no-brainers.

When Derek leaves, I don't say *one, two, three*. I don't employ patented techniques of discipline. Nor do I turn and head the other way.

I simply hit replay on his last words.

Come find out.

I listen to those three words over and over, letting them ripple through my body, linger on my skin, and turn me on and on.

It's like he's flipped open the lid of a jeweled chest of desires, and he's luring me with his invitation to explore the treasures inside. I want to know everything it holds. I want to head upstairs, turn the corner, and find him in bed.

I want to discover him, and to find *us*, because I'm dying for him.

But there's more than mere lust at stake—that, I

can manage on my own, thanks to fingers and wands and twelve-speed friends in my nightstand drawer.

This is different.

This is a longing deep in my bones. It shows no sign of leaving. Because I care for him so damn much.

I like him for more than the body, the face, and the jawline. I like what's inside. I like what he says. I like who he is.

Maybe that makes the trek upstairs a dangerous idea. In fact, it probably is. But I don't want to play games anymore either. Taking a deep, fortifying breath, I leave the kitchen, cross the back hallway, and open the door to the stairwell.

I stop at the bottom stair, letting my eyes adjust to the dark. I know these steps. I've walked up them. But tonight, they seem to lead to a whole new world. An after-hours den where passion is the offering, where pleasure is the currency, where coming together is the one and only goal.

In my black heels, I take the first step.

Then the next.

With each click of my shoes, I shed my worries. I dismiss the hurdles—*he's my roommate, I need to focus on work, I'm not interested in relationships.*

I kick over those roadblocks as I go.

We're mature adults, and we're choosing *this* tonight—we're choosing the feel-good factor—and all its risks. I'm choosing what I've wanted from the start. I wanted all of him in the waffle truck.

I reach the top step, and it's silent. So quiet and still. I listen for his breath, for a word, a groan.

All I hear is my own hammering heart. I keep going, turning the corner into his room—a wide-open space with a big bed and moonlight streaming through the windows.

He's lying on top of the covers, eyes closed, hands parked behind his head.

I half expected to find him with his hand wrapped around his cock, shuttling his fist.

But he's waiting.

Like he promised.

Waiting for me. Wearing his jeans and T-shirt.

It's my turn. It's my move.

I make it.

"I found you," I say into the dark. It feels like I'm speaking for the first time in my life. Like words have eluded me till this moment.

His eyes float open, landing on me. Even from across the room, they're blazing with lust. "So you did."

Kicking off my heels, I glance around. He's barely moved in. "I like what you've done with the space," I say, joking.

He pats the bed. "This is the best part."

I stare at him for a minute, taking in his long legs, his strong thighs, his flat stomach, and the scruff covering his jaw.

He gazes back, his lips a straight line. It's still my turn. He's shown his hand. The rest of the night belongs to me, and I have to decide what cards to play next.

I go all in, pushing every chip to the middle of the

table as I slide off a strap of my dress. Trembling, I ask, "Will you take off your shirt?"

He's up in an instant, tugging his T-shirt over his head in that sexy way men do, tossing it on the floor and stalking over to me.

Roughly, like I want it, he grabs my head, curls his fingers around my skull, and tugs me close. "Get all your clothes off, kitten. I need you naked, and I need it now."

In a flurry, we're pulling, tugging, unzipping. There is no slow dance, no striptease. I push down the other strap of my dress and take it off, while he unsnaps the button on his jeans then shoves them down, kicking them off.

My eyes eat him up, savoring the visual feast of his body. His strong arms covered in art, his firm pecs, his insanely defined abs. And then *there*. The birds on the V that leads to what I want. His hard-on strains against the fabric of his black boxer briefs, showing off the most delicious bulge I've ever seen.

My mouth waters, and I ache between my legs. My hand darts out, cupping him.

He growls. "You like that, kitten?"

"Love it," I murmur as I stroke his hard length. But as much as I savor touching him like this, I want him in the flesh. I push down the waistband, and he shucks off the briefs the rest of the way. His cock is beautiful. Long, thick, hard. Pointing at me.

He gazes at my breasts, barely hidden in lavender lingerie. "Look at you. Just fucking look at you." He stares at the demi-cup lace bra and tiny matching panties, fire flickering in his brown irises. "I knew you wore panties like this. I almost don't want to remove them, but I have to get you naked."

"Please. Just rip them off, Derek."

He grins, like I've given him the keys to the kingdom. "No way am I ruining these beauties. They're too pretty."

But he's fast anyway. Or really, we are together. I flick off my bra and he tugs down my panties, ogling me like a hunter staring at his prey. "You're so fucking stunning. I want my mouth all over you. I want my cock inside you. I want my hands *everywhere*."

I grab his jaw and drag my fingers over his trim beard, loving the rough stubble. "I want all of that, but right now can you just please fuck me and put me out of my misery?"

His smile is wicked and carnal. "Nothing would make me happier than to rid you of all that aching pain of wanting me."

He slides a hand between my legs, and I whimper, dropping my chin against his shoulder. "*Derek*," I moan as his strong fingers glide across my slickness. I'm on fire, desire crackling through my veins, igniting my entire body.

Groaning, he rasps out, "This is what I want. All this wetness all over me. You're so slippery, kitten. So fucking wet. So fucking hot for me."

I shudder, rubbing against his fingers, rocking into his hand. "Don't tease me with your fingers. Just take me."

He steps away, grabbing a condom from the nightstand. "Get on my bed where you belong and spread those gorgeous legs for me."

A second later, I'm on my back, my legs parted for him. I prop myself on my elbows as I watch him open the wrapper. "Is this how you want me?"

He groans appreciatively as his eyes roam over me. "I want you every which way. I want you on your back, on your belly, with your ass in the air. I want you in the shower, up against the wall, and I want you riding my dick."

My eyes light up.

He rolls on the condom. "You like that last one?"

"I do. But I want you to control me. Can you do it like that?"

"Kitten, I can fuck you from beneath you, no problem." With the protection on, he winks and falls to his back on the bed. "Get on me."

I climb over him, straddling his big, strong body. He holds the base of his cock, and I position myself over him then sink down.

I shudder as he fills me.

I'm so wet, he's all the way inside me in an instant. He grabs my hips, groaning. "You're delicious. So tight on my dick."

Hot tingles spread across my body, darting over my shoulders and sprinting down my arms as I linger on the intensity of taking him in. He's so deep, I swear I can feel him stretching me. He takes the reins, grabbing my hips. With his fingers digging firmly into my flesh, he thrusts up into me, hard and rough.

Even though I'm on top, he's fully in charge,

guiding me up and down with a rhythm so right, so intense, I know it won't take long. I'm riding him, but he's fucking me, and I'm racing toward heaven.

Knowing that, feeling it deep in my bones, I let go. I let him do all the work, jutting up his hips, stroking into me as I thread my fingers through my hair, moaning and panting.

"Kitten," he growls. "You're so fucking sexy like that. Touching yourself. Playing with your hair. Let me see you touch your tits."

I part my lips on a pant and slide my hands down my body, cupping my breasts.

He pushes up harder, faster, deeper. "Yeah, do that. Squeeze them. Tease your nipples."

Pleasure coils in my belly as I knead, as I squeeze, while he strokes up into me. My gasps grow louder, more frequent, and his thrusts turn more frantic. He keeps fucking up into me as I lose myself more and more to the sensations, to the utter intensity of this moment in the darkness of his room.

Desire and lust radiate down my spine, ripple to my toes. Pleasure consumes every cell, and I want to fall into this moment, to ride this sensation to the edge of the Earth.

"I'm close," I whisper.

"Let me get you all the way there." With his hands still on my hips, he spreads his fingers wide enough to stroke my clit with his thumb.

And the second he does, I know I'm gone.

I've hit the point of no return, and I'm galloping toward the cliff.

I see the strain in his jaw, the intensity in his eyes. He gazes at me with a longing I've never seen before. Like he's as lost to this pleasure as I am. Like there's never been sex like this before and we're the only ones who've ever felt this wild, this intense, this connected.

That's what I see in him. That's what I want to keep seeing, again and again.

"So fucking sexy," he murmurs as his thumb slides over me, and I shatter.

Coiling, tightening, sinking *onto* him as I shake, the orgasm pouring its bliss from a pitcher, covering every inch of me. I fall against his chest, wildly bucking, coming apart, shouting incoherent noises of ecstasy.

He grabs my ass hard and pumps up at a fevered pace. Before I'm even aware of what's happening, he flips us over, moving me to my hands and knees. He drives into me, pushing his hand on my back. I lower my chest to the bed, lifting my ass, and he goes to town. Owning my body. Taking his pleasure. Giving me more. I'm boneless, mindless, melting into another orgasm that pounds relentlessly through me as he finds his with a feral roar. "Coming. Coming so fucking hard."

Growling, he unleashes himself, and it's wild and crazed and the sexiest thing I've ever heard.

It's everything I wanted it to be.

It's everything great sex should be.

And I don't want it to end. I don't want us to end. I want more and more of him.

That's the trouble. He's in, far and deep, and my want for him has only multiplied.

25

DEREK

Perri clears her throat, shooting me a most serious stare. "Are we going to talk about the elephant in the room?"

I give her a sideways glance. Damn, she looks good curled up next to me, her red hair spilling over my chest. Absently, I stroke a few strands. "Elephant? What elephant?" I let my eyes stray down my body. "Oh, are you talking about my trunk?"

"Perhaps I am." She wiggles her eyebrows, tap-dancing her fingers along my abs, making her way to my dick, which is on a well-deserved five-minute sabbatical.

"Ah, so that is what you want to discuss. Go on."

Her fingers tease my pelvis. "Well, yeah. You just gave me two fantastic Os with this magnificent dick. I would like to take a minute to talk about how magnificent it is."

Grinning like a cocky bastard, I park my hands

behind my head and preen. "Sure, absolutely. I can listen to you praise my dick all night long."

She runs her hand along my thigh. "Let me put it this way: it's everything I hoped it would be."

I smirk, meeting her naughty gaze. "You've been thinking about my dick, haven't you?"

"Uh, yeah. Just like you've been thinking about all my lady parts," she says, shimmying her hips from her spot next to me in bed.

"Busted. I spend an inordinate amount of time thinking about all your parts." I tug her closer, savoring the way she fits in the crook of my arm. I drop a kiss to her silky auburn hair. I'm going to enjoy the hell out of my access to her at last. My freedom to touch her, kiss her, explore her. "So tell me, how else have you been objectifying me?"

She roams her eyes up and down my body, and as she does, a new awareness hits me. She's not running down the stairs. We're not making awkward post-screw conversation. She's not hemming and hawing as she tries to get out of my room. She's lying next to me, wrapped in my arms, and we're talking. I didn't plan what would happen after we slept together, but I like that *this* is the thing that happened naturally.

"Well, I definitely fantasized about your body. It is kind of crazy-hot. You know that, right?"

"And you better know that you're wildly sexy. Also, I'm glad you like what you see," I say.

She squeezes my biceps. "Let's be honest. You're a fine specimen. Like, you could be in a zoo somewhere."

I laugh. "You're going to put me in a zoo?"

"Yes, a man zoo. If there were one, you would absolutely be the most popular exhibit. All the women would be coming to check you out. Men too, probably."

"And in this man zoo, would I be naked, or would I get to wear . . . I don't know . . . say, a thong, or a fig leaf?"

She taps her chin and stares at the dark ceiling. "It would depend on the day. If I ran the man zoo, I would make a schedule." Her fingers travel along my chest, stopping at my pecs. "On Mondays, you'd wear a fig leaf." They ladder down to my abs. "On Wednesdays, you'd wear a thong." They jog to my hips. "And on Fridays, it would be nude day, because everyone knows Friday is the best day of the week."

"And would Fridays be the most popular day at the zoo?"

"Absolutely. The lines at the man zoo are so long on Fridays because everyone wants to get in. But tickets are hard to come by."

"Makes sense. I'd be a prized exhibit. Tickets would be bartered on StubHub. Wait, do I do a show at the zoo? SeaWorld-style or anything?"

She shoots me an inquisitive stare. "Do you have any talent? Can you dance? Do backflips? Catch fish in your mouth?"

"I'm a killer dancer. Do you want me to dance for you right now?"

She arches her brow as if she's thinking about it, then she cuddles closer, settling deeper into my arms.

"No, I kind of weirdly like snuggling with you, so please don't get up and dance," she says.

"Aww, you like snuggling with me. Admit it—you like me." As soon as the words spill out, I freeze. Was I supposed to say that she liked me? Is that what this is about? But hell, maybe it's become that. Because I like this woman so much that it's well beyond like. It's moved to the next level.

She raises her face, but her expression reminds me of her aviator shades. It's practiced and gives nothing new away. "I just let you bang me after we played a massive resistance game. I think it's obvious that I think you're the cat's meow."

She didn't quite answer my question. But I'm not entirely sure I was asking it the right way.

I switch back to an easier topic, since I don't think she wants to venture down this *do you dig me* road. Come to think of it, I'm not entirely in the mood either. That's not what we're supposed to be about anyway. This is an itch we're scratching, and she's made it clear from the start that she has no interest in a long-term scratching partner. Nor do I.

"Let's talk more about this snuggling," I say, keeping it light. "Tell me why it's weird that you like snuggling with me. Is it weird that you'd like banging me and snuggling with me?"

Nervousness flickers across her eyes. Gone is the stoic gaze when she answers, "Banging, no. Snuggling, yes. It's kind of weird to like it. Don't you think?"

And maybe that wasn't an easier question at all.

Neither one of us quite knows if we're supposed to be snuggling, or if we're supposed to be yanking on underwear, waving goodbye, and saying, *Thanks for a great screw.*

I do my best to ease the tension once and for all. "It's not odd in the least. I'm an awesome snuggler." I demonstrate, tugging her closer and dropping kisses to her forehead, her hair, her jawline. Because fuck weirdness. Screw labels. I like having her in my arms, plain and simple. We don't need to discuss it. We can just do it.

She sighs happily, relaxing again and reminding me it's best if we keep whatever this is on an easy level. "So you're good at snuggling, you're willing to participate in my man zoo, and you have a magnificent dick. You're a prize, Derek."

I blow on my fingers. "You haven't even mentioned my awesome sandwich-making skills or my chicken stir-fry talents. See? I do have special abilities for my man zoo exhibit."

"You sure do, because you're pretty amazing in the kitchen." She pats my stomach. "And watch it. If you keep talking about food, I'm going to make you go whip something up in the kitchen."

"And would you wait here for me?"

"Would you serve me in bed?"

"If you wanted me to, I'd serve you in bed."

Because I want you to stay here so I can have you again, I think to myself.

Propping herself on an elbow, she returns to exploring my body, her fingertips trailing over the ink on my arms. "What's the story with all your tattoos? When did you get them?"

She continues tracing the canvas of sunbursts. This is a conversation that's easy to have. I don't need to worry about hidden meanings or the secret language of women. "As soon as I turned eighteen," I tell her.

"You were jonesing for ink?"

"Absolutely. I've always been drawn to it. Probably because my father had a lot of tattoos."

"What did he do?"

"He was an EMT. Like father, like son. He actually took me to get my first tat."

Her chin drops. "That's unusual."

"I know, but he said if I was going to get one, he wanted me to go to the best, to a shop he trusted and an artist he liked."

"And which one was the first design?"

"The sunbursts."

"What do they mean to you? Do they represent anything special?"

"Good question. They can mean a lot of things, but in most cases, and for me, they mean life and energy. And that's what I want to focus on. Both in my job and in how I live every day. Fully, with light and with vitality."

She smiles, the kind of smile that spreads nice and slow, like she's enjoying learning this detail. "I love it. I love that it's not some dark reason. But it's one that matters to you. A personal mantra."

"Exactly."

She draws her fingers over the bird silhouettes. "These are sort of unusual. Why birds?"

"Birds are awesome. Think about it—how much would you like to fly?"

Laughing, she answers, "Flying would be rad."

"Exactly. Whenever someone asks what your superpower would be, flying has to be up there on the list. Wings are the best. They give you freedom to make choices."

She tilts her head, raising a questioning eyebrow. "What held you back from making your own choices? Did you have a good relationship with your parents?"

I smile, glad I can answer that one painlessly. "I had a great relationship with them. I'm a what-you-see-is-what-you-get kind of guy. As for the birds, I believe in freedom, but I don't mean it in some crazy gung ho way. I mean, we should all be free, all humans. To pursue our dreams, to be the best people that we can be, to live in peace."

"I like peace," she says in a Californian surfer drawl. "Is it odd being a cop who likes peace?"

"No. I would imagine that's exactly why you're a cop."

"Sometimes I wish we weren't needed, but we are, and I feel like ultimately that's what I'm striving toward. To keep the peace."

"Did you always want to be a cop?"

She nods against my chest. "Arden, Vanessa, and I used to play cops and robbers, and I was always the cop."

"You were never the robber?"

She shakes her head. "Never. Not once. I remember this one time, they pretended to break into a jewelry store, but it turned out Vanessa was the owner and needed the insurance—"

She stops talking, blinks, and says, "Holy shit."

I sit up straight. "What is it?"

She stares at me, her eyes widening as she sits up in bed too. "I think I know who broke into the jewelry store a few months ago."

My brow pinches. "Vanessa?"

She shakes her head, then launches into a rocket-fast explanation of a jewelry store theft that has bedeviled the chief. But she gives no details about who she thinks is behind it.

"I'm not following. Should I be following?"

Laughing, she shakes her head. "No. I can't go into the specifics, but I think I've got it figured out."

"Do you need to go write this down? Call the chief? Or go arrest someone?" I roam my gaze down her bare body, savoring her curves and praying she won't have to leave my bed anytime soon.

She points at the dark window. "Yeah, I'm going to go knock on doors and haul in bad guys right now."

"Put some clothes on first, will ya?"

"Yes, that's it. I'm going to interrogate suspects in my birthday suit."

"I like your birthday suit."

She narrows her eyes. "Want me to interrogate you, then?"

I let my eyes stray downward to my crotch. "You can interrogate me with your sexy mouth, officer."

"Don't you worry, Mr. Trouble. I will do that soon enough."

I gaze up at the ceiling and press my palms together. "Thank you, Lord."

Rolling her eyes, she nudges my waist with her elbow. "There's no rush on the investigation. I'll deal with it tomorrow and discuss it with the chief when I see him."

I tap her forehead. "Also, since you mentioned my magnificent dick, can we talk about this magnificent brain? The way you put that together right now in the middle of a conversation about cops and robbers was damn impressive, kitten."

She mimics me from earlier, blowing on her fingernails.

"I mean it. Watching you crack the case was hot. Though that might be because you're naked in my bed, with that just-been-fucked look. Incidentally, you wear the just-been-fucked look quite well."

"Do I?" Her voice dips into sexy, smoky territory.

In response, my dick heads to the land of the upright. "You wear it spectacularly well." I trail my hand down her side, groaning appreciatively at the intoxicating feel of her soft flesh. "Hey, Perri?"

"Yes?" Her voice is vulnerable.

We're side by side, and she looks at me as I run a hand along her hair. "You're beautiful."

She smiles shyly, and I've never seen her look like that, but it suits her. That hint of sweetness, that touch of demure. "So are you."

In that moment, with the moonlight slicing

through the windows, with the night wrapping around us, something shifts. We've stripped off the teasing; we've removed the barbs and the jabs. And we've given in to the physical.

But this second goes further. It feels emotional. It feels possible, like we could be more than two housemates who are hot for each other.

Trouble is, I don't know how we stay on this level. I don't know if she wants to.

With my gaze locked on hers, I swallow then ask an open-ended question. "So where do we go from here?"

She throws it right back at me. "Where do you want to go?"

And maybe this is the snuggling question all over again. Maybe it's best if we focus tonight on the horizontal.

"I feel like you're not out of my system." The words don't quite come out like seduction. They come out like the truth. They have a double meaning, although I suspect the bedroom definition is easier for both of us.

"I feel like you're not out of my system either." She punctuates her words with a soft, barely-there kiss. A kiss that seems to reveal that maybe we're on the same page.

But pages like this are hard to stay on when you're not entirely sure.

They're hard to stay on, too, when you're hard.

She wraps a leg over my hip.

I yank her body against mine, bringing her closer.

"So, should we try to get out of each other's systems a few more times?"

Her eyes are flirty, giving me the answer I need for now. "I think that's a really great idea. You do make me feel pretty damn good."

"I can make you feel good again, kitten."

"Is that so?"

"I can definitely give you more of the feel-good factor."

Her eyes sparkle. "I'll take it. Why don't we work on feeling good till the kissing contest?"

I smile. "It's a deadline."

"It's a deadline," she repeats.

A deadline and a deal.

I roll her to her back, put on a condom, and do everything I can to get us out of our systems.

26
PERRI

Jansen points at me, shaking a finger in admiration. "You're brilliant."

I beam as we talk in his office the next day. "That sounds possible, doesn't it? An inside job?" Excitement blasts through me as I review the details I didn't share with Derek last night.

From his spot behind the desk, Jansen lifts his coffee cup, nodding as he drinks. "Sounds not only possible, but likely."

I tap the desk. "And insurance money has to be the motive."

"I agree with you there. I'll review it later, but good work on this, Keating."

"Thank you, sir."

I leave his office, walking on sunshine and hope.

For the rest of the day, I have to force myself to stop smiling. To wear my serious cop face as I finish my patrol work. But inside, I swear I can taste the promotion. I'm reaching for it. I feel it in my grasp.

When I leave the station that evening, I'm the one bopping down the steps, and it's not because of a viral video or a dance move. It's because I might have proven I'm the best man *and* the best woman for the job.

I don't feel an ounce of guilt for going after the promotion and trying my hardest to nab it. I flash back to Derek's advice from the other night. He was right. He kept me focused. He kept me from spiraling into a worry that's far too common for women. And I'm damn grateful because I love my job and I love this town.

I head straight to Helen's Diner, where I'm meeting the girls. Vanessa and Arden have already snagged a booth, with menus spread out in front of them, even though we all know every item by heart.

I'm glowing when I reach the table and stand before them with arms spread like I'm about to make a pronouncement.

Arden studies me. "My, my. Don't you look like the cat who ate a couple of tasty canaries?"

I thrust my arms in the air in victory. "They were delicious canaries, because I'm pretty sure I just cracked a case."

Vanessa cheers then offers a hand to high-five. I smack her palm and slide in next to her. "It's *CSI* Lucky Falls–style," Vanessa adds.

"You know it." I take a deep breath. "Also, I'm

going to tell you something that's going to literally *not* shock either of you one bit."

"Your brother is driving you crazy?" Arden offers.

"You bought more olives?" Vanessa suggests.

Arden goes again. "You finished knitting the pink sweater in one evening on account of sexual frustration?"

Vanessa takes her turn. "You're hungry?"

I laugh at how they've nailed me on every single point. But still, that's not what I want to tell them, so I roll my eyes. "It's like you don't even know me. I'm seriously disappointed in both of you. Try *harder*," I say, emphasizing the last word.

Arden's brown eyes bulge. Vanessa's jaw drops, and she shoves my shoulder. "You didn't?"

I wiggle my shoulders. "I did. I slept with Derek last night."

"How was it? Scale of one to multiple orgasms?" Vanessa asks.

Arden snaps her gaze to Vanessa, giving her a *you can't be serious* stare. "Look at Perri's face. It screams *so satisfied*. I'm betting she had a lot more than one."

I grin wildly as I hold up three fingers. "Twice the first round. One in the second. It was literally the best sex ever in the entire universe."

Vanessa squeals. "Tell us everything."

I give them more details, but I don't share everything. I don't tell them how Derek's dark eyes lingered possessively on me the whole time. Nor do I tell them how intensely he talks to me, how he looks at me like I'm the only woman he's ever wanted this much, this deeply. I don't share how he cuddled me like it was the most natural thing in the world to do. And I definitely don't say how much that snugglefest made my heart squeeze with a strange new happiness. With wonder. With a sprinkle of possibility.

After we order and the server brings waters, Arden adopts a more serious look. "How on earth do you plan on balancing all of this? Doing the roomie, and having him as the roomie? Are you guys actually going to be together?"

I scoff. "No. He doesn't want a relationship. Nor do I." I shrug, keeping it light. "We've agreed we'll get this sex out of our systems until the kissing contest next weekend, and then we'll move on."

Vanessa chokes on her water, nearly spitting it on the table. "Are you kidding me? You think that's possible?"

"Of course. It's absolutely possible. We're adults. We can do this like adults. We said we would."

"But how do you do that?" Vanessa presses. "How do you turn it off?"

I imitate turning a knob. "You just do. There's no other choice."

"Keep telling yourself that, sister."

"You don't think I can?"

Arden chimes in, "I don't think *anyone* can. But I also think *you* actually like him."

Vanessa adjusts the way her turquoise-and-red twin sweater set falls on her shoulders. "I think you passed Like Street twenty miles ago, sweetie. You're cruising down Falling Hard for Him Highway. Now you've added great sex to the route? You're pretty much on a one-way road to a relationship. Not that I'd know. It's been a long time since I traveled down that lane."

Arden pats her hand. "There, there. You'll get to Hot Sex Town soon enough. You're just taking the back roads." My blonde friend turns to me. "But I second everything Vanessa says."

"I'm not on a road to anything but winning the contest." I fold my hands together. "Speaking of, how are you girls doing with your charity projects? All our birthdays are coming up soon, and Vanessa is doing a wine and bowling competition for fire relief. What about you, Arden?"

She sears me with her dark eyes. "I'm doing great. I'm starting a 'round up your purchase to the nearest dollar' campaign for children's literacy at my store. But don't think you can change the subject."

"But I thought our projects were the subject," I say coyly.

"Your project has moved well beyond charity," Vanessa adds.

"Just be careful," says Arden. "You started this because you were attracted to him. Then he moved in and you felt you had to shut off the faucet of lust. But now, all of a sudden, the faucet is running full blast."

"Faucets, roads, kissing contests. It's all good," I say, waving a hand airily. "We have a deadline and a deal, so it'll be fine."

"Just be careful. You're so tough on the outside, and I get it—you have to be for your job." She reaches across the table and lightly pokes my belly. "But you're really a softie."

I wiggle away. "We'll be fine. Neither one of us wants anything more."

Vanessa lifts a doubtful brow. "You say that, but do you still mean it?"

I lift my chin, choosing to mean it. Needing to believe it. "Of course."

But there's an ounce of a doubt weighing on the back of my mind, and it's becoming heavier.

Because last night was more than just pent-up desire. It was more than three orgasms.

Derek and I didn't simply snuggle postcoitally, all casual and we-can-handle-this cool. We snuggled until the sun rose, when he stretched those ropy arms over his head and dropped a morning kiss to my forehead. I whispered a hoarse *good morning* before I hopped out of bed to go to work.

It was the feel-good factor and more, because he makes me feel good physically *and* emotionally.

But I know that temporary hot sex is all it can be. And really, I remind myself, that's all I want.

When I arrive home later, after a workout and a shower, at least there's no doubt what I want when I find this note on the chalkboard:

Your room. 10 p.m. Get out your cuffs or a scarf.

27

DEREK

She chooses the scarf.

"Tell me why you picked this," I tell her as I tie the silky green fabric around her wrists and to the bedposts.

"Because when you use cuffs on me, I want the fur-lined kind."

When. I love that she says *when*. I tighten the knot. "Then I better get you some furry cuffs, kitten. For tonight, this'll do."

"It'll definitely do." Her voice is breathless. Her body is breathtaking. She's lithe, long, and willing.

Eager too.

Still fully dressed, I crawl over her and lower my mouth to her neck, pressing a soft, tender kiss to the hollow of her throat.

Gasping, she arches beneath me. I brush my lips down her body, over her throat, through the valley of her breasts, detouring to her tits, with their rosy nipples tipped up and begging for attention. "Last night," I rasp against her skin, "you made me fuck you hard and fast to put you out of your misery."

She moans as I suck on a nipple. "You wanted it too."

I let go and leave a trail of kisses down her belly, lavishing attention all over her skin. My God, she tastes intoxicating. "I did. But tonight I want to take my time, like I promised the day I met you."

She whimpers, lifting her hips, asking for more. "You're cruel."

"I'm terrible," I whisper as I reach one delicious hipbone then lick.

"Oh God," she moans, and I grab her hips, keeping her in place.

"I'm going to spend my sweet time pleasing you. I'm going to take as long as I need to devour your body. I'm going to get drunk on your taste, kitten."

"Tease." She strains against the scarf, and I smile wickedly, pleased as sin. I plan to pleasure her till she cries out again and again.

"It's only a tease if I don't deliver, and I'll deliver." I kiss the top of her curls, and she bows her back, moaning my name. My cock throbs against my zipper, begging to be set free. All in due time. This is about her. This is about giving her the pleasure she deserves. Because she does. She's sexy and sarcastic and sassy, and underneath all that, she has a soft heart and a sweetness that I fucking . . .

I stop myself from even thinking about what I feel for her. I part her legs and focus on the physical as I inhale deeply her addictive scent. "You smell delicious."

"Why don't you get closer?"

I look up, grinning, loving how much she wants this. She's gazing down at me, desperation in her eyes. "I'm pretty close," I say, though I'm inches away.

"Please," she whispers.

"Aww, you want me to lick your sweet pussy right fucking now, don't you?"

She lifts her hips, seeking my mouth. "*Yes.*"

I kiss her right thigh, groaning as I make my way down to her knee.

"*Derek,*" she moans.

"Ask again."

"Please go down on me."

I move to her other leg. "One more time. Tell me one more time."

She cries out in frustration. "Go down on me. Please, go down on me now. Go down on me this goddamn second."

I lick my way up her thigh, reaching the apex, and then I gaze at her face. "Spread your legs. Spread them nice and wide for me. Show me how wet you are. Show me how much you want my mouth on you."

She takes no time parting her legs wider, her knees falling open, giving me unfettered access to the paradise between her thighs.

My hard-on hammers against my jeans. This woman. Fuck, she glistens for me. "God, you're so sexy it should be a crime."

"But it's not, so just please, please, *please* go down on me."

"If you insist." I dip my face between her legs, and I draw one lingering line up her wetness. My eyes float closed, and I groan in tandem with her. "Fuck, you're delicious."

She tastes like salt and sin, like honey and lust. She's so fucking wet I want to bury my face in her juices.

So I do. I lick and I kiss and I suck. I can feel her all over my chin and my jaw, and it's intense.

"Oh God," she cries out, bucking and thrashing.

Holy fuck, she's thrashing already.

I reward her passion, fucking her with my tongue. She moans. "So good, so good."

And I make it even better when I add a finger, crooking it deep inside her.

She practically shoots up off the bed, then she grinds down on my fingers, fucking them as I fuck her pussy with my tongue and lips and fingers.

Soon we're both growling like animals, losing our minds with pleasure till Perri shouts my name, spreading her legs even wider and rocking against my face.

She comes gloriously, flooding my tongue with her sweetness, her screams of pleasure bathing my ears. Her climax is the stuff dirty dreams are made of. I kiss her softly till she comes down.

She's smiling, grinning like a dopey fool, when she opens her eyes and issues a husky demand. "Give me your cock."

And I'm all too happy to oblige. I stand, shuck off my clothes, and bring my hard length to her lips. I let her lick the tip, and I grunt because the sensation of her tongue on my dick is out of this world.

"Are you going to fuck my mouth while I'm tied up?"

I stare darkly at her. "Don't tempt me."

"Is that what you want? To fuck my mouth while I'm like this?"

I shake my head. "No, kitten. I want you down on your knees, because I want to wrap my hands in your hair while I fuck your mouth."

She shivers, and I know she wants it too. I untie her, and she scrambles to the floor. In seconds, she's taken me deep.

Pleasure shoots through me instantly, running wildly through my cells, spreading to every inch of my body. Perri sweeps her tongue up and down, then swirls it around the head. Bringing her closer, I fill her mouth, thrusting into her as she sucks me so hard, I can't see straight.

I don't want to see.

I want to *feel*, and feel I do when the most intense orgasm blasts through me as she tugs on my balls, making it so fucking good, and I come in her throat.

After, I tug her into my arms and kiss her. She kisses me back with a brand-new ferocity. In seconds, we're wrapped around each other, arms, legs, hands. We're a tangle of limbs and heat. She kisses me deeply as I tug that lush body against mine, my hands exploring her, hers exploring me as we kiss madly. We kiss for minutes, for hours, forever, it seems. I can't stop kissing her. I don't want to leave her room. Don't want to stop what we're doing. Not tonight. Not tomorrow. Not in the near future.

But at some point, I do break the kiss, because the need for words becomes more powerful. "I couldn't stop thinking of you today."

Her lips part. Her eyes lock on mine. "It was the same for me."

I kiss her again. "You're in my head, kitten. I thought about getting you naked again all day long." But that's not even the half of it. I thought of her—all of her.

"All day, Derek. I wanted to touch you so badly. Wanted to kiss you."

And it's not lust that radiates in my bones right now. It's something much more powerful. Something deeper. "I fucking love kissing you," I whisper, because that's all I'll let myself say.

"Kiss me all night."

I tuck my finger under her chin. "Sleep with me again."

She meets my gaze with her naughty one. "I was planning on that."

I shake my head. "No. I mean spend the night with me. In my arms. *After.*"

"Yes. I want that. I want you."

Soon I'm inside her again, and it's spectacular, even better than last night. I have to wonder if we're having the kind of sex that will only get better. If it's the kind that shoots through the roof as your feelings escalate, because I'm pretty sure the roof is the direction my feelings are headed.

The next morning, I get out of bed first and make her breakfast, and the look on her face when I serve her eggs and toast makes me feel like I hung the moon.

This pride makes me want to do it again for her.

And again and again.

Every damn day.

28

PERRI

Derek might be fantastic in bed, but he's awful at bowling. He knocks down three pins on his last turn, keeping us firmly in the caboose spot we've earned. He shrugs and shoots me a lopsided grin as he strides back toward me at Vanessa's bowling alley. We're out with our friends a few nights later, like we had talked about doing.

"Can't win 'em all." He brushes his fingers against my arm.

"Or any, by the looks of it," I tease.

"At least I'm good at other things." His voice is a sexy whisper as he gazes seductively at me.

"You're very good at all those things."

Gabe clears his throat as we separate. "Our turn to hammer the nail in your coffin."

Arden laughs, squeezing his arm. "Sweetie, don't gloat in front of them."

"Should I wait till we get home before I gloat?"

Laughing, she answers, "Exactly. Save the gloating till they're out of earshot."

"Anyone ever mentioned that you two are sore winners?" I toss out at them.

Because that's the other issue with bowling. We're going up against both Hunter and Shaw, who are killing it, and Gabe and Arden, who are even better. Those two are some kind of bowling power couple. I suspect it's because they've been partners for more than a year, and before they started to go out, bowling was some kind of sublimation while they spent a year flirting with each other.

Arden takes her final turn, knocking down all ten pins. Gabe pulls her in for a kiss. "You're so hot when you bowl your little ass off."

She wiggles the butt in question and drops a kiss to his cheek. "And you're so hot when you bowl spares like you did on your last turn. Because I don't want you to forget I'm still beating you even though you're on my team."

He drops his jaw. "Wait. You're competing against me when we're playing together?"

"Of course. I've amassed sixty-five percent of our points."

"Woman, don't make me show you up in *Words with Friends* later," Gabe warns.

She cups his cheek. "You'd never do that."

He tugs her in for a grind-and-bump style of hug. "I absolutely would."

I mime gagging. "Guys, do you want me to arrest you for indecent display of public affection?"

Arden shrugs happily. "I'm willing to go to jail for that."

Gabe plants another kiss on her lips. He adds sound effects as he smooches her. Then he dips her.

"Get a room," Shaw shouts.

"Get it now," Hunter puts in.

"You're all just jealous," Gabe tosses back at the guys.

Derek leans close to my ear. "I'm not jealous. Because I know where your room is."

I smile at him as tingles race across my skin. This man is a non-stop flirting machine.

"How's the kissing practice going?" Shaw asks us, as he lifts his bottle of beer, taking a drink.

Hunter jumps in. "Wait. Let me guess. Based on the volume of ass smacks, stupid grins, and giggles between these two tonight, I'm betting it's going just fine. Am I right?"

It's no secret that we have a thing going on. It's never been a secret, because of the kissing contest. But only my girls know there's something more, and Arden keeps quiet. Vanessa's not in earshot. She's manning the bar at the alley tonight and chatting with her sister, Ella, who's keeping her company. Finley's there too. She's a friend of ours from the next town over.

Derek turns to me, his dark eyes twinkling with mischief as he answers Hunter's question. "Is he right? Or is he so fucking right?" He gives me no time to respond, since he cups my cheeks then brushes his lips against mine. My eyes float closed, and I expect a soft, tender kiss, but it's hot and passionate, and it might very well send the temperature in the whole damn alley soaring as he claims my mouth.

Arden's no longer quiet. She's hooting. Gabe is clapping. My brother and Hunter are now directing their "get a room" shouts at us.

But I don't care because I'm aching for Derek from one unexpected kiss.

He breaks it but keeps a hand on my arm to steady me. I look into his eyes, and they're locked on mine. "You're right. You're so fucking right," I murmur.

"And fucking is what I want to be doing very soon."

I shudder. "Me too."

I'm ready to grab him and tug him out of here when my brother shouts out like an Olympic judge. "I give you a two. The technique is all wrong."

I groan and shoot him a dirty look, then a feminine voice cuts in from the bar. It's Finley. "That was a nine point five. I might even base a kiss in my next show on that," she says, and I give her a thumbs-up, since I'd love to be the inspiration for a kiss in the TV show she pens.

Vanessa chimes in. "I beg to differ. That kiss was a perfect ten." She's heading toward us, one of her swing dresses swishing at her knees. She's carrying a tray full of beer bottles.

"I'm giving them a ten too," Arden says as Vanessa sets the tray on the table. Shaw stares at Vanessa the whole time.

What the hell? Does Shaw have laser vision on my

friend now? Shaw tips his chin at her and whispers *thank you* as he grabs a beer.

She smiles back at him as she turns to go. "Need anything else?"

I blink, unsure of what's going on with my brother and one of my best friends.

"As a matter of fact, I do. Be right back," Shaw says, but before he can join her, I grab him and tug him a few lanes away.

"Is something up with you and Vanessa?" I whisper.

He scoffs. "Please. You told me years ago if I went near either of your best friends, you'd have my balls in a sling."

I widen my eyes. "I said that?"

He raises his right hand in an oath. "It was eleventh grade, and you declared both your besties off-limits, then reinforced it with a threat to the boys. I shudder at the memory."

"I was sixteen. How do you remember that?"

He clutches his crotch. "I take the fate of my balls quite seriously, thank you very much." He gestures in Vanessa's direction as she returns to the bar. "I'm simply helping her with her wine and bowling shindig. So there. Cool your jets, little sis."

I breathe a sigh of relief. "Good. Because you're kind of a ladies' man, you know that?"

"Kind of? The ladies love me, and I love them right back. Also, speaking of balls, looks like you're getting your lady balls off."

I swat him. "*Shaw.*"

He waves me off. "I told you it'd work out just fine with the two of you living together. And I was right. You're perfect roommates. Neither one of you wants anything serious, and you're both getting along while getting it on."

The last person I want to discuss my sex life with is my brother, so I shoo him off. "Go. Be on your way."

He tips an imaginary hat and takes off, while I noodle on his parting words. Derek and I do get along well. We get along great.

I'm not a fool though.

I might play the tough girl with my friends, but inside I'm aware of the risks with Derek. I'm aware of the possibility that . . . whatever this is . . . could go belly-up before our end date.

And even if it doesn't, it'll end.

It'll end.

But as I gaze at Derek while he chats with Hunter, Gabe, and Arden, the last thing I want is to stop.

* * *

We leave together in my car.

As I pull onto the road, Derek fiddles with the radio. "You don't want Shaw to be with Vanessa?"

"How could you tell?"

He laughs. "Maybe by the way you pulled him aside and seemed to read him the riot act after he ogled her?"

"He did ogle her, didn't he?" I ask, flicking on my turn signal as I slow at a light.

"Looks like she ogled him too though. Hate to break it to you."

I shoot him a withering glare. "I'll pretend you didn't say that."

"So I was right. You don't want them to be together?"

"He's kind of a player. But I also don't think there's anything there. They've known each other for twenty-four years, and it's not like anything has happened before."

"Sounds like they've had twenty-four years, then, for the connection to slowly burn."

I set a hand on his forehead. "Yes, you do have a fever."

He squeezes my thigh as I head down the next street. "You suffer from denial."

"He's just Shaw being Shaw. He's flirty with her sometimes. That's all."

"And she's flirty right back. You notice that, right?"

I shoot him an admonishing look. "Derek, I adore you and your ability to cook and give me multiple orgasms and bowl as terribly as I do. But you are not allowed to discuss the possibility of my brother being with one of my best friends."

He laughs louder. "Why not? It seems like he's really into her. And it seems like she's really into him."

"It can't happen."

"Why?"

I swallow roughly and think of the answer. "Because she deserves the world. She deserves the best man possible."

"Isn't that your brother?"

"I love him fiercely. I'd go to war for him. But Shaw is a goofball and a supreme ladies' man. She needs somebody who's going to treat her like a queen. That's what she deserves. Also, if you keep discussing my brother, you're going to turn me off, when ten minutes ago I was picturing you bending me over the bed. Do you really want that on your conscience?"

He mimes zipping his lips.

* * *

After we head inside, he wastes no time. He takes me to his bedroom and our clothes come off in record time.

"Turn around. Bend over the bed. Get your ass in the air."

I lower my chest, pressing my elbows to the mattress, fashioning my body into an L. He reaches for my wrists, stretching my arms above my head, then kisses his way down my spine. I squirm and moan as he flicks his tongue along my back, teasing me to the point of exquisite torture. I'm hot and wet and already moaning. He's hard and ready and practically grunting.

He slides a hand between my legs, slipping a finger inside me, and I rock against his hand. "You're always so wet for me, kitten. So slick and ready for my fingers, my cock, my tongue."

"You turn me on so much," I breathe as he adds

another finger, then thrusts deeper. "You've had me like this all night."

"I can tell, and I fucking love it. I love how wild you are for me." He crooks his fingers inside, sliding another one across my clit, and I scream in pleasure, tossing my head back, careening toward the edge already.

"Yes," I cry out.

"Fuck, Perri. I love watching you come. The way you let go. I want to feel you come on my hand any fucking second."

And he nearly has his dirty wish. I don't quite come on command, but I'm quick. Several hard, fast thrusts of his fingers hitting just the right spot, and I detonate.

I don't even have time to come down before he's driving into me. I cry out again from the sheer intensity of his thick cock sliding deep inside.

"Yes. This. You," he mutters, his voice smoky. "I've never wanted anyone like this." He punctuates each word with a thrust. "Never."

His words send me soaring. "Me neither."

Another thrust. "Yeah?"

"I want you so much," I pant.

He grinds into me, harder, farther. "So fucking much, kitten. So fucking much."

"Same. It's the same for me."

He drapes his chest over my back, telling me to keep my hands above my head, stretched out on the mattress.

He grinds against me, taking me, having me,

making me feel wildly insane with pleasure as he growls in my ear, whispering filthy words.

So fucking hot.
Love your sweet pussy.
So tight.
Love the way you grip me.
Love fucking you.

Soon I'm coming again, and he's chasing me there, our shouts mingling in a chorus of sweat and ecstasy.

The best part isn't the orgasm that rocks my world. It's the way he wraps his arms around me, kisses my neck, and tells me I better spend the night in his bed again.

Somewhere out there, a warning sign flashes, telling me that all these nights together will zoom us straight down Feelings Street. But I ignore it, maybe because I'm already there.

* * *

I ignore it, too, because the moments with him are wonderful. After he brings me into his arms, he runs his fingers through my hair. "Thanks for taking me out with your friends tonight."

"They're your friends too."

"I know. But I still appreciate it."

"Did you have a good time?"

"Yeah, I kinda like this town."

"You should think about staying," I whisper. But I don't say the next thing. I don't mention where he's going to stay or what happens when this month ends, if we keep living together or if something gives. Instead, I flip around and change the subject, wincing as I say it because of the reminder of the ticking clock. "So, that kissing contest next weekend?"

"Yes, the deal, the deadline," he says, and it almost sounds like it pains him too to think of it.

"We only have a handful of nights left to practice kissing."

"Don't remind me," he mutters then nuzzles me, kissing me like he can't stop, like neither one of us is trying to meet the screw-till-we're-out-of-our-systems deadline.

Even so, I need to pick a category for the contest by tomorrow, so I pull apart from him briefly. "What category do you think we're best at?"

He brushes his finger against my top lip. "Seems we've always been good at the most passionate one. We would make everyone jealous, you know that?"

I tremble. "I do know that."

"Doesn't it feel like no one has ever kissed the way we do?"

The tremble turns into a full-body shudder. "It feels that way."

He drops a soft kiss to my lips, and I wriggle against him. "Like nobody else could kiss this passionately."

"It's felt that way since the first time you kissed me."

"It makes me want to keep kissing you," he says, and he does.

He kisses me nearly all night long, and in the morning, it still feels like I didn't get enough. He's not any closer to being out of my system than he was a few days ago. In fact, he seems to be even deeper in it.

So deep, there's a four-letter word for it.

29

DEREK

I shoot a few hoops with Travis at the park on my day off on Monday.

I make a beaded bracelet with Molly in their backyard.

And Devon spends a whole lot of time working out her mouth on a teething ring. By the time seven thirty rolls around, I'm whistling a happy tune as I stroll down the street with the three monsters I love.

Because life is fucking good.

The job is firing on all cylinders.

The kids are well-adjusted, and Jodie's managing her hubby's deployment with my help.

The nights, though, are the best part. Perri and I have fallen into a rhythm of work, work out, eat, screw, sleep.

Later? Rinse and repeat.

Nothing like great sex to make a man feel as if he

walks on water. And with Perri, I'm speeding, skiing, and boogie boarding over waves.

Nothing can get me down. Not even when Jodie calls and asks if I can hang around with the rug rats for another hour so she can finish her invoices. Absolutely, I tell her.

"Can we watch a movie, Uncle Derek?" Molly asks when I hang up.

"I want to see *Wreck-It Ralph*," Travis adds, flashing the winning smile that nearly always gets him what he wants.

"What do you think, Dev?" I inquire of the little blonde baby hanging in the BabyBjörn on my chest.

She coos her agreement.

Since I'm a few blocks from our house—I mean, Perri's house—I head up the steps with the kiddos and knock on the front door.

With her red hair swept up in a messy bun and a curious glint in her eyes, Perri sweeps open the door. "You don't have to knock."

I gesture to my plus-three. "It's the front door. That's your domain. Plus, I have a crew with me."

Molly pushes forward. "Perri, can we watch *Wreck-It Ralph* in your house with Uncle Derek? We'll be good." She bats her eyelashes.

"We promise we won't be too loud," Travis says, making the case too and pressing his little palms together.

Devon gurgles.

And Perri? Her smile is golden, like she's lit up inside and glowing.

"Twist my arm, why don't you?" She sweeps the door open.

She grabs her knitting from the table and stuffs it into a bag next to the sofa.

We pile into the living room, find the movie on Netflix, and stream it on the TV. The kids climb onto the couch with Devon in Molly's arms, Travis wedged to my side, and Molly glued to Perri. That also puts the gorgeous redhead smack dab next to me, where I want her. We're thigh to thigh, knee to knee as we watch.

I send instructions to my body not to get turned on while watching a flick with the kids. For the most part, my body listens dutifully.

But there's an organ that doesn't listen so well.

And it's not the one between my legs. It's the one in my chest. Because Perri's answering questions from Molly all through the movie, then letting my niece cuddle up next to her while she holds the baby, then making funny faces.

The next thing I know, Molly asks what Perri's been making.

"A little knit cap for Devon. But shh, don't tell her," Perri whispers.

"It'll be our secret," Molly whispers in return.

And my heart slams against my chest. It thumps harder, faster.

She's making a gift for my sister's kid.

Plus, she was completely cool with the surprise of three little six and under stinkers showing up on her couch tonight.

What's more, I knew she'd be cool with it because that's who she is. I'd never describe her as laid-back, but she is a roll-with-the-punches kind of gal. She's unflustered and completely chill.

She also has one hell of a huge heart under that fiery exterior.

As the movie nears its end, I watch her and Molly, enjoying the little whispers, the smiles, the laughs. My heart races, beating a thousand times faster, and my skin heats in a whole new way.

This woman is not out of my system.

She's not only a fantastic fuck.

She's not simply a fine roomie with temporary benefits.

She's the woman I'm falling so damn hard for that it's scary. Much scarier than the horror novels I read.

But like those, I can't seem to stop turning the pages.

* * *

Near the end of the movie, Perri rests her head on my shoulder. Her eyes are fluttering. I press a soft kiss to her forehead, and she murmurs something then slumps against me moments later, snoozing.

She sleeps through the credits, stirring when Jodie arrives later to corral the kids. She stretches and says hi to my sister. "Your kids are darlings."

"They have their moments. And I can't thank you enough for helping out."

"All I did was point the remote at the right flick," she says with a smile.

"Not true," I chime in. "You chatted with Miss Chatterbox the whole time."

Perri smiles. "It was a blast."

"You also willingly let us pile like a pack of puppies on your couch," I add.

"Well, I like puppies, so it was no problem," Perri adds, then turns to Jodie again. "We had fun. Also, your walnut blue cheese bread is the best."

"Come by this weekend, and I'll give you a loaf."

She waves a hand. "I'll buy it."

Jodie shakes her head adamantly. "Your money is no good at my booth."

I help Jodie out to the car, load up the kiddos, and kiss them goodnight. My sister closes the doors, walks around the car, and crosses her arms. "You did it."

I knit my brow. "Did what?"

Shaking her head, she smiles that knowing big sister smile. "You fell for her."

"Did not," I say, lying through my teeth.

"You can't fool me. What are you going to do about it?"

That's the million-dollar question with the far-too-frustrating answer. "There's nothing to be done. She doesn't want a relationship, and I don't either."

"I don't believe you. You're in love with her."

I wince. Hearing the stone-cold truth spoken aloud makes all these crazy emotions feel even more real. I definitely don't have the time, space, or inclination for this level of feeling, but it's fucking here, making itself known. Trouble is, I'm not sure how to deal with it, because I don't want to get hurt again. "There's nothing to do," I say firmly. "But I love you. And good night."

"Good night, Derek. I love you too."

I go inside, doing my best to leave the conversation and all its dead ends behind me. Perri's stretched out on the couch. She smiles up at me, her eyes fluttering open.

"Hey, gorgeous." I bend over her, pressing a kiss to her forehead. "Are you tired?"

With a yawn, she answers, "Long day."

"Let's get you to bed."

She shakes her head. "Not yet."

"Why not, sleepyhead?"

"I need something first."

My heart lurches with hope. "What's that?"

She reaches up for me. "You."

And I'm ready to go. Damn, my dick likes her all sleepy and sweet.

And my heart does too. That dumbass organ leaps out of my chest and lands next to her, curling up, finding its home.

Fucking hearts. Fucking dicks.

I can't resist her with either one.

I join her on the couch, grabbing her jaw, and pressing a soft kiss to her lips that turns hungry, greedy. She yanks me closer, stripping off my shirt, unzipping my jeans.

Her clothes come off too, and in seconds, she's spread her legs, inviting me home.

I grab a condom, cover myself, then slide inside, gasping at the indescribable pleasure of the warm, welcome feel of her.

"Mmm," she murmurs, wrapping her arms around my neck.

I groan as I rock into her, moving slowly, taking my time. I go deeper, and with each lingering thrust, she moans and whimpers, sounds that pull me further into her orbit. That tug on my heart. Every noise of pleasure makes me want to get closer to her in every way.

She lifts up her knees, moving her legs higher, letting me go deeper into her. So deep, so far, so intense.

"God, it's so good with you," she murmurs against my neck.

"So fucking good."

She nibbles on my ear, her breath sweet against my skin. "It's never felt like this."

I shudder. "I know. Not with anyone."

And it hasn't. I've never felt this way, this wild, intense connection. As I move in her, bringing her closer, looking into her eyes, that connection crackles like electricity. I know she has to feel it too.

The way she stares at me with such trust, with something that damn near feels like love, almost makes me say something.

I bite my tongue.

"You're so quiet tonight," she whispers as I swivel my hips and rock into her.

"I just like looking at you."

"I like it too."

I stare into her eyes, overcome, overwhelmed, until the physical becomes too intense and pulls me under its crashing, pulsing wave.

We reach the finish together.

And all I know is that I don't want this to end. Because I'm in love with her, even though it's scary as hell. Even though I don't want to get hurt. Even though I didn't come looking for this.

The worst part is I don't think anything will come of all these emotions swelling inside me, because *in love* is where she doesn't want me to be.

30

PERRI

As my Thursday shift draws to a close, I head to the break room, log in to the online entry for the kissing contest, and tap the button for our category.

As I snag a Diet Coke from the vending machine, I hit submit on my phone. Jansen strolls past, heading to the coffeepot. "Most passionate?"

Damn, he has eagle eyes. Good thing I wasn't looking at anything private. It's an even better thing I placed my lingerie order at home last night.

I tuck my phone into my back pocket and grab the can, cracking it open, acting as nonchalant as I can be. "That's the plan."

I hope my response comes out casual, but I can hear the hint of embarrassment in my voice. I don't want to discuss kissing with my boss. More specifically, I don't want to discuss passionate kissing with the man who signs my paychecks. Talking about entering the contest when it was a mere idea was one thing. Now it's a reality, and it feels weird.

I shrug and take a sip. "Seemed like an easy one."

"Is it?" He wiggles his eyebrows. "Seems like it'd require a lot of practice."

A blush creeps across my cheeks. I swallow roughly as I try to fashion an answer. Am I supposed to say, *Hey, don't worry, I've been spending my nights practicing?* Or *wait till you see how jiggy we can get?* Did I cross some strange line by entering the contest at all, or by entering in that category?

"Should I switch to something else? Maybe sweet?"

"Hell no. Theresa and I don't need that kind of competition. I'm just impressed you entered in most passionate."

"I could change to another category?" I offer, but the question, and asking it again, comes across as meek. I want to kick myself for asking it. I sound wishy-washy. I don't sound like someone who's tough on criminals.

He smiles, the teddy-bear grin that he's known for. "Just giving you a hard time, Keating. You know I think it's great that you're doing this." He grabs his cup of coffee and leaves.

I down a thirsty gulp of Diet Coke, wishing it would calm my nerves.

It doesn't, and I'm honestly not sure why I feel any nerves. Except I can't help but worry that I've overstepped somewhere, somehow.

I return to my patrol, walking the streets in the

town square. When my shift ends, I bump into Elias on the steps leading out of the station.

And he's not bopping this time. He's grinning, and his smile reaches the stars.

"My, my, someone is happy," I say, grateful for a distraction.

Elias's eyes dance with delight. "Happy doesn't even begin to cover it."

"Did you win the lottery?"

"Feels like it." He punches the sky. "I got it."

I tilt my head, inquiring, "What did you get?"

"Chief just told me I'm going to be a sergeant. I landed a promotion." He taps his chest. "Me! Holy shit! Me! I can't wait to tell the missus. She's going to be so proud of me."

I blink, shock slamming into me, making it hard to breathe. He can't be saying what he's saying. Please don't let him be saying that. "You did?"

Shaking his hips, he dives into a whole new kind of dance. A victory jig. "And I didn't even need a viral video to do it. Chief just said he was proud of my track record and I'd earned the job. No need for theatrics. Just good, honest work."

I draw a harsh breath and will myself to show nothing. Display nothing. "That's the way to do it," I say robotically. But underneath, a knife of self-doubt slices away at my heart. Did I take on too much with the extra reports? Did I botch the jewelry store case? Was traffic duty a mess? A new issue lodges in my mind—was it a mistake to enter the contest?

But I can't wallow in my worry. I have to care.

Elias is my friend, and he wants this. He's earned it. I should be thrilled for him. I slap on a smile. "I'm so happy for you. You deserve it."

I give him a quick hug.

"Aww, thanks, Keating. What about you?"

"What about me?" I ask, dropping into my cool-as-a-leather-jacket mode.

"Were you going for it?" he asks, sounding worried on my behalf. I can't take a chance that his concern will morph into pity for me.

I wave a hand, admitting nothing. "Please. It went to the best man. I'll see you later."

Quickly, I race to my car, yank open the door, and slide inside. I jerk on the seat belt, my throat jamming with stupid emotion.

I swipe at my cheeks, erasing any evidence of sadness as I turn on the engine and pull away. I gulp back the idiotic tears as I drive. But they won't listen to me. They keep threatening to spill free. I turn the corner and pull over at the sidewalk. I do something I can only do when I'm finished at work.

I cry.

And I hate myself for it.

I should be happy for Elias and his family, but I'm selfishly sad for myself.

I shouldn't care this much.

But I feel like I failed.

Like maybe I didn't deserve it in the first place.

Maybe I was focused on the wrong things.

I blink back my tears and stare at the dashboard.

I should go find my girls, drown my sorrows in a

glass of wine the size of my head, throw darts at a board, and then drink some more.

But I don't call them because for the first time in forever, they aren't the ones I want to turn to.

Derek is.

I want to find him, tell him, ask him to wrap his strong arms around me. Feel him smooth my hair, kiss my forehead, and say, *Don't worry, kitten, you'll get the next one.*

I want him to kiss away my sadness, to hold me close, to let me know he's there for me even if the job isn't.

Gulping, I look in the rearview mirror at the sad, unexpected truth reflected in my eyes. I want all that because I've fallen in love with my housemate.

I'm head over heels for the man.

But what if he's the reason I didn't get the gig? What if love made me lose my edge?

What if I took my eyes off the prize?

The questions stab at my brain as I head back on the road and drive home. By the time I reach my house, I've arrived at several new conclusions.

Falling in love distracted me.

And falling in love was indescribably dumb.

Derek made it crystal clear from the start that he's not interested in a relationship.

That's why there's only one thing to do.

31

DEREK

I don't always remove marbles from noses, but when I do, I'm awesome at it. "Stay still. I've got it."

Thanks to forceps fixed firmly in place, the small blue marble slips out easily from the tyke's nose and into my waiting palm.

"Oh, thank God," the mother says, relief flowing off her in waves. "You're a lifesaver."

She turns to the three-year-old with the predilection for testing his nasal cavity. "Don't ever scare me like that again, Oliver." She grabs her son and tugs him in for a crushing hug, the kind that won't end for days.

"I won't, Mommy."

"He's going to be just fine," I tell the worried woman, who called mere minutes ago.

"You're a godsend. How can I thank you?"

"No need to thank us. It's our job, and we're happy to do it."

She extends a hand. "I'm Claire. I work in events at the Windemere Inn. If I can ever do anything, let me know."

Something about the name of her workplace tugs at my memory, but I can't quite place it.

"Derek," I say, then introduce Hunter. "And don't worry. We are all good."

Hunter offers her the marble. "Want to keep it as a memento?"

Claire laughs as she hugs her son closer. "No, I want him to never play with marbles again."

"I won't play with them, Mommy."

"Take care, and hopefully you won't need us again, but you know where to find us if you do," I say.

We head down the stairs of the apartment building. "If only all our calls were that easy."

Hunter drums his fingers against the banister. "But I'll take easy when it comes our way. And it's been an easy day."

"Couldn't agree more. Today is just one of those fantastically good days."

As we reach the van, he shoots me a curious stare. "I'm not sure I'm buying that marbles are the reason for your happy mood."

I yank open the door. "Why not?"

He scratches his jaw. "Call me Sherlock, but I think you might be one happy camper thanks to a certain lady cop."

I smile as I get into the passenger side.

Once he's in the driver's seat, he turns to me,

pressing the issue. "You two were putting on quite a show at bowling the other night."

"Glad you enjoyed our special performance. Be sure to tune in again every night."

"Every night, is it?"

"Hey, you want lunch?"

"Dude, it's ten in the morning. Even I'm not hungry just yet. Don't change the subject. Are you guys a thing now?"

I shrug. "I don't know."

He turns on the engine and pulls away. "You might be slow on the uptake, then. If I were you, I'd get on that right away. I've known Perri Keating for years. I can't tell you the last time she dated anyone."

That intrigues me to no end. "That so?"

"She's pretty much a solo rider. But man, she's a catch. That's why if she were into me, I'd make damn sure no one else had a chance."

The mere prospect that any other man might look at her with desire makes me snarl. "No one does have a chance."

"Oh, it's serious, then?"

"No," I grumble.

"Then make it serious, dickhead. She's a special lady."

* * *

Trouble is, I don't know how to make it serious. All I know is we can't exist in this in-between state forever.

The kissing contest is this weekend, and we made a deal. We set a deadline.

Sure, I could tell her I've revised my stance. I could let on that I'm ready for her to be mine and only mine.

But if I'm going to do what Hunter said—make sure no one else has a chance—I need to figure out when and how to make my case.

Relationships aren't my strong suit. I'm more than rusty, and even though flirty banter and dirty phrases fall easily from my lips, words vex me when it comes to what to say to a woman who's declared relationships off-limits.

When I return home that night, open the back door, and turn into the kitchen, I find a note on the blackboard.

For the baby.

Next to the blackboard is a gift, wrapped in pink paper with a bow. *This woman.* My God.

How can I convince her to be mine when she doesn't want to be?

I don't fucking know.

But I *have* to figure it out.

My ears zoom in on the sound of water running. She must be taking a shower. As I regard the empty kitchen, I figure food is always a good start with Perri.

Peering into the fridge, I spot broccoli and mushrooms. I start chopping so I can sauté the veggies for her, along with some jasmine rice.

As I'm cooking, the shower stream cuts off, and I hear the telltale signs of her moving around her bedroom. A few minutes later, she emerges, entering the kitchen wearing her witch jammies and a black tank top.

My heart stutters.

Holy hell. She's so damn beautiful and . . . sad? Her eyes are rimmed with red, like she's been crying. What the hell?

"Hey, kitten. What happened?"

Her mouth is a straight line, but then her lower lip quivers. "I didn't get the promotion," she whispers quietly.

"Shit, babe, I'm sorry." I turn off the burner, setting down the spatula.

I reach to hug her, but she winces and holds out a hand. Stops me. Whispers *one, two, three*, then jerks up her gaze. "How long are we going to do this?" Her tone shifts instantly from sad to tough as nails.

"Do what?"

She flaps her hands wildly. "Play house? Cook and screw and pretend we're a couple?"

For a long time, I want to reply, but tears spill from her eyes, and I'm thoroughly confused. I don't know what to say or how to say it or if now is the time.

"I like cooking for you." As soon as that comes out, I'm positive it isn't what she needs to hear. But I'm also certain I've no clue what to say to fix a damn thing. I try again. "How long do you want to do this?"

She swipes a hand across her cheek then takes a deep breath. "We agreed to do this till the contest. Get it out of our systems. But we're acting like a couple."

Wait. I'm wrong. *This* is the time. *This* is my entrée to wedge my way into her heart. "We are. That's true."

That's a start, right?

She frowns. "But we're not. You know that?"

"I do know that," I say tentatively, trying to figure out how to keep moving the conversation forward.

She points at me. "You made it clear from the start. You said *no relationships*. You said you didn't want anything. And now we're living together, and we can't just keep going on indefinitely. You're my roommate, I'm your landlord, and the more we keep doing this, the stupider we get."

I blink, trying to process why we're dumb.

She sucks in a breath, and her voice catches again as it rises. "And it's distracting. It's totally distracting."

"It is?"

She flings up her hands, her eyes shining with tears. "Obviously it's distracting. I didn't get the job, and that means I'm not focusing on work enough. All I think about is you. Seeing you and being with you and kissing you and talking to you." She snaps her gaze away, covering her face with her hands. "And it's stupid. It's so stupid because we made a deal."

Carefully, I step forward, peeling her fingers from her face. "You think you lost your focus?"

She swallows roughly, nodding. "I've been laser-focused on this forever, but then you showed up and look what happened. I missed the biggest chance of my career."

I hardly know what to say.

I barely know what she needs.

I don't know how to make this right.

But if she were an emergency call, I'd have to figure it out.

Once I apply my work problem-solving skills, the answer flashes before me.

Brilliantly and awfully.

She needs an out. She needs an end.

I have to give it to her, as much as it hurts.

I'm not simply ripping off the Band-Aid. I'm tearing away a piece of my heart that she inextricably owns.

But that's the only way to fix her emergency. I look her in the eyes, staying strong, treating her like a patient who needs help, who needs a calm and competent guiding hand. "Maybe we should cool things off. What if we go back to being housemates? Like we agreed. Does that sound good to you?"

She closes her eyes like everything hurts.

And everything does hurt.

Every damn piece of my heart and soul screams at me. But I have to give her—and us—the treatment we need. "We can also call off the contest if you think that's best."

Her eyes snap open, and I expect a fiery answer. Something like *No way, we're going to nail it, and then we'll go back to being roomies.* Instead, she shrugs. "I don't know anything anymore."

My fingers itch to soothe her, my arms to wrap around and comfort her. But I remain unyielding as a statue. "Sleep on it, Perri."

She seems to flinch when I say her name. Maybe because she's used to being *kitten*. Maybe because I can't call her that anymore.

"I'll sleep on it. But you're right about everything else. Housemates—that's all we can be."

The pain radiates through me, but I know she's hurting too. I add, just to be sure, just so I give the patient exactly what she needs, "We'll go back to how it was."

"Yes. There's no other choice."

I want to tell her there are a million other choices. There is being together, there is falling in love, there is taking care of each other.

But she's not in this the way I am.

And I'm not in it now either.

She leaves for her room, and I finish cooking, but when I take a bite, the food tastes like dust. I clean the dishes, grab Devon's present, and carry the hat for my niece upstairs, wishing it didn't feel like a parting gift.

32

PERRI

I punish myself with Pilates on Saturday morning. It's fitting, since I have to twist myself into a pretzel and abuse my core to no end.

But it's worth it. Need to stay in tip-top shape for my job.

Wait.

I should revise that philosophy. I need to get in better shape for the job. Physically, mentally, emotionally. I'm too soft. That's the problem. I have to erase all my emotions. I'll dive deeper into work, spend more time on cases, take some classes. I'll work endlessly on improving all my skills. I need to be the best, and then, since I work in a male-dominated area, I simply must be better than the best.

That's the only way for a woman to succeed in a balls-deep field—by going above and beyond, and then beyond even that.

I crunch, bend, and contort myself through the

rest of the class. The workout ends, and still breathless, I turn to Vanessa and Arden. "I think I'll stay for a second class."

Arden's eyes widen in confusion, then shock, then misery. "Seriously?"

I pat her shoulder. "You don't have to hang around."

Arden flicks her gaze to Vanessa, and they exchange a knowing glance and a couple of nods.

Arden stretches her neck. "Oh, I do have to stay, and I hate morning exercise."

"I'm fine," I say. "I can totally handle a second class solo. I know you're a grumbly Garfield in the morning."

"I'll stay too," Vanessa offers like she's volunteered to be a tribute in the Hunger Games.

"I'm fine, I swear. You don't have to stay." I stand to grab my water bottle and down a thirsty sip.

"But we do," Vanessa chimes in, adjusting her ponytail. "Because if you're staying, it means you're mad at yourself."

I scoff as we shuffle toward the studio door. "Please. That's not the case."

Vanessa grabs my arm. "It is precisely the case. This is what you did in eleventh grade when you didn't get into AP History. You decided you weren't tough enough, so you started practicing more for soccer. It didn't even make sense."

"I thought if I was in better physical shape, I'd be in better mental shape. It made perfect sense," I say, defending my sixteen-year-old logic.

"It doesn't make *any* sense," Vanessa says firmly, "and you know it."

Arden nods vigorously. "It's your weird, twisted punishment brain at work."

"I don't have a punishment brain," I whisper furtively as I close the top to my water bottle and step into the hallway as the class files out.

"You do," Vanessa says. "When something doesn't go your way, you whip yourself to go faster or work longer."

Arden squeezes my arm. "You did something similar a few months later when you were convinced your SAT scores sucked. You buried yourself in SAT-test prep books for days on end."

I squint, cycling back more than a decade. If memory serves, my strategy failed. I didn't raise my score at all on the second sitting of the test.

"But that's not what I'm doing now," I protest. "I'm simply trying to . . ."

I don't finish the thought because a messy stew of emotion wells up in my chest. Regret tinged with disappointment, mixed with a deep longing for that man—feelings that brew and simmer and threaten to boil over.

I can't contain them much longer. I point to the studio, like I'm going to head back in. "I'm just going to . . ."

But the words come out choked, as if there are pebbles in my mouth.

"Perri," Arden says softly, grabbing my wrist. "Are we really doing this? I hate morning exercise, but I love you more. I will stay if that's what you want. But we can also go somewhere and talk. You know, *talk*." Her eyes hook with mine, and hers are soft, full of compassion. "Talk is that thing you do with your best friends."

She looks at me with such love, such unconditional loyalty, that I can't keep it together anymore. I burst into tears in the studio.

All I want is to talk to them.

All I want is to share my feelings.

And because they're the best friends I've ever known—the best friends anyone has had in the entire history of the world—they usher me out of there before I make a complete fool of myself in front of the ladies in the class.

33

DEREK

It just motherfucking figures that after the last twenty-four hours I'd draw another shitty hand for the overnight shift

First, we're dispatched shortly after midnight to a rural area after a house fire. The fire department is already on scene.

We arrive too late, and I feel so goddamn helpless. A candle left burning caused the fire, and the man is dead. Next, a motor vehicle collision twenty miles away steals our attention. Hunter and I turn on the sirens, and when we arrive, the cars are tangled together in a metal mess. We hightail it to the hospital and arrive in the nick of time, rushing the most critical patient into the ER.

Please let us help this one.

"I hope we got him there fast enough," I mutter as we head to the van after handing off to the docs and nurses. "I'd like to do some good rather than keep coming up short."

"I hear you, bro. I couldn't drive much faster. I'll say a prayer that it was fast enough."

But will it be?

That's the question that hangs over me today. Is anything enough? Is there anything I could have done differently with Perri? Anything I could have said the other night to change the course of that wretched conversation? Our talk was like a plane running out of fuel, sputtering from the sky and crash-landing in a charred heap.

I've no clue if there was a different button I could have pressed, a different route I could have taken.

As we continue through the night, I hit replay for the fiftieth time on our talk. But still I have no answer.

* * *

With darkness still blanketing the sky, we respond to a call from a well-to-do home. A woman's boyfriend rings 911, saying he fears she's having a heart attack. She's young and healthy. Thirty-six. Jodie's age. "Most likely a panic attack," I say as we drive, hoping desperately that's all it is.

"Definitely. That's what it usually is," Hunter says, staying chipper. God knows I need it.

We arrive with the fire department not far behind.

But we don't stay long.

Because she's not suffering from anxiety. This is the real deal.

We rush her to the ER, and I hope and I pray and I plead for someone, anyone to look out for this woman who could be my sister.

She's too young to go. Too healthy—on the surface—to be heading to meet her maker.

Anxiety claws at me for the next few hours, and I do my best to keep it at bay as we tend to other calls. I need blinders something fierce today.

"You okay?" Hunter asks at one point.

"Just thinking about my sister. She's the same age."

He sighs sympathetically then claps my shoulder. "She's in the best hands possible, that woman."

I nod, trying to believe she'll come through. "She is."

"Let's just keep doing what we can, okay?"

"Definitely."

But an hour later, when we're back at the hospital, dropping off a skinny dude who had a bad fall at work, one of the nurses tells me the thirty-six-year-old didn't make it.

My throat squeezes. "For real?"

"Yes."

I wince, wishing fervently she was delivering some other sentence. This cruel news winds its way through me, tightening every muscle, squeezing every organ.

I tell myself she's just a patient, just a call, just another day.

But this one hits closer to home. Maybe I'm raw already from last night with Perri. Or maybe it's the pile-on. Whatever it is, my heart is leaden. My feet are heavy, and all I have left to hope for is that the car accident patients from earlier are okay.

The nurse says they're stable, and that gives me some glimmer that I'm not a grim reaper, spending a day collecting souls.

When I find Hunter at the ambulance, his face is tense. "What's the 411?"

"She's gone," I say, gritting my teeth.

"I'm sorry to hear that."

"Me too."

Even though she has nothing to do with me. I don't know her from Eve. But this loss is shoving its way under my ribs and setting up camp in my chest.

Battered and bruised when I leave at the end of the shift, I mutter a toneless good night to Hunter before I hop on my bike and head home as the sun rises.

Only, I don't want to go home. It doesn't feel like home anymore.

All I want is to see Perri, talk to her, tell her about my day, and then get lost in each other and forget what went down for me and what went down for her. Just be there for each other through the shitty times.

Curl up with my woman, get close to her, and reconnect to the living, to everything that makes us keep going in these jobs that can drain us dry.

I want to smell her hair, kiss her skin, and feel like she's my reason.

But there's a big fat problem. She's not my woman. She doesn't want me to be her man.

I drive past her house. It's hers, not mine. I head to see Jodie.

34

PERRI

"You're going to get another shot at another promotion," Arden says, encouraging me in the way only she and Vanessa can. "I know it."

We're sequestered in the back booth of Helen's Diner, away from the handful of others here at this early hour. "You're right," I admit, wiping away the last tear I'm going to let fall.

"It sucks that this one didn't happen. But there might be politics or who knows what involved," Vanessa adds. "Look, I run my own business. So does Arden. The reality is there are a million things that go into these decisions, and sometimes we make the right ones as bosses and sometimes we make the wrong ones. And sometimes things just happen in their own time."

I nod, my heart rate settling, my self-loathing dissipating. Vanessa makes a good point. The reality is, I'm good at my job. I simply didn't get this promotion because—I didn't get it. Not because of Derek, and not because I was distracted. I wasn't distracted at work. Someone else earned the job. I take a deep breath. "It's silly to get so worked up. I should be happy for Elias."

Arden tucks a strand of blonde hair over her ear. "You can be happy for him and be disappointed for yourself. The two aren't mutually exclusive."

"Exactly. You're not required to operate your emotions like you administer the law. Emotions aren't black or white, right or wrong. Sometimes we feel twenty-one emotions all at once," Vanessa says, laughing as she spreads her napkin on her lap.

I manage a small laugh too. "I think I'm feeling twenty-five emotions."

"Sounds about right," Arden says as the server swings by, bringing us our breakfast.

We thank her, and as I dive into my eggs, Arden clears her throat. "But I don't think it's the disappointment over the job that's the main reason you're upset."

I meet her gaze head-on. "It's not?"

When we arrived at the diner, I told them everything that went down last night—the promotion, how I felt awful for not being happy for Elias, how my missing out on the advancement was clearly related to Derek, and how Derek and I decided it was time to end our silly little roomies-with-benefits deal. A deal that *always* had an expiration date.

Vanessa shakes her head, drinking her coffee. "Maybe the reason for one of those twenty-five emotions—sadness—is that you don't merely *like* Derek." She takes a beat. "You love him."

I wince and struggle once more with the astonishing sharpness of that truth. How do people live with these pesky feelings wreaking havoc with plans all the damn time? "I did fall in love with him, but it's not going to work out. I'll be fine. I'm always fine."

Vanessa presses. "But why do you have to be fine?"

"Because nothing is going to happen with him." The words taste like gravel, and it hurts to say them. I don't know how much longer I can keep up the *everything is all good here* routine.

"How do you know for sure?" Arden asks.

"He doesn't want anything," I say tightly, keeping my tone as neutral as I can, as if this fact doesn't rip apart my heart.

Vanessa taps her finger on the table. "Who cares about him? What do you want?"

I heave a sigh and scoop up another forkful of eggs. "Right now, I want to stop feeling sorry for myself."

My brunette friend stares sharply at me. "You're a strong, independent woman, but you don't have to be so independent all the time."

"Lean on us," Arden adds.

"Let us be here for you," Vanessa seconds.

Just like that, awareness clobbers me.

Sometimes it takes your girlfriends—no, your best friends—to help you see what's surrounding you. Supporting you.

They are.

They're my people.

They're my family, my sisters. Whether I have Derek in my life or not, these women will always be here.

And lately, I haven't let them completely be who they want to be—my best friends. It's time I let them be my best friends in word and deed. I'm going to lean on them like they want, and like I want.

I crack open my chest and let out the truth. "I do love him. I did fall in love with him. And you two were right all along, warning me, looking out for me, and being here for me, even when I wasn't leaning on you."

"That's what we do," Vanessa says. "Look out for you."

Arden laughs sweetly. "And we do it especially when you're pigheaded."

Sighing, I manage a smile. "I am pigheaded. God, I'm the most stubborn mule there ever was."

Vanessa raises her coffee mug in agreement. "You won't get any argument from me."

I inhale deeply, feeling like I can breathe for the first time in more than twenty-four hours. Feeling like I don't have to navigate all these thorny issues solo. "I should have told you two about my worries over the promotion. I went to Derek instead." It comes out like a confession.

"Was he helpful?" Arden asks carefully.

I flash back to our conversation in the kitchen. "He actually was. He's easy to talk to. He's very straightforward, very tell it like it is."

Vanessa smiles. "Sounds like I'd have approved of whatever advice he gave you."

"I think you would have, but let's not talk about him right now. Let's do something else. Something we haven't done in a while."

"Pillow fight?" Arden offers.

I stick out my tongue, shaking my head. "Love you madly, but no thanks. I'm thinking we get out of town."

Vanessa rubs her palms. "There's a new vintage shop on Fillmore Street. I've been salivating over the tea length dresses in the online catalog."

"Let's go to San Francisco," I say, and my smile spreads across my face, it stretches along my arms, and it reaches my toes.

Arden lifts her mug. "I'll drink to that. You need to spend the day with your best friends. You're not going to exercise away the problems."

Laughing, I take another bite. "I'm definitely not. But you know what?"

"What?"

"I'm not going to wallow in them either. I'm moving on. So what if I didn't get the promotion? So what if I didn't get the guy? I have you two." I set down my fork and speak deep from the heart, like I've been doing. "I need you guys. I love you both."

"We love you," Arden says.

"And we're always here for you," Vanessa says.

There's only one thing to do now. Group hug. I have my sisters, and I'll always have them.

When we're done, we climb into Vanessa's car and

wind our way through town. But as we pass the Silver Tavern, I shout out that it's time for a pit stop.

"You want to go wine tasting at nine in the morning?"

"No, I want to snag a little something."

I pop into the restaurant that's open for breakfast and lunch, buy a gift card, then a card at the pharmacy on the next block.

We stop at Elias's house on the way out of town. I leave the card tucked into his screen door, congratulating him on his promotion and giving him and his wife a chance to dine at their favorite lunch spot to celebrate.

35

DEREK

I grab Jodie and wrap my arms around her the second I see her. "So good to see you."

"Whoa. You okay, sweetie?"

I nod, grateful her heart is beating. "Just glad you're alive."

"I'm not going anywhere, but it sounds like you had a bad day."

"You can say that again." I let go and pinch the bridge of my nose, squeezing hard like I can erase the night.

She glances inside. "Travis, watch the baby. I'll be back in a minute."

"Yes, Mom!"

She steps onto the porch and shoots me a serious stare with her dark-brown eyes. "Want to talk about it?"

I shake my head. "Not really. Just one of those days. Know what I mean?"

She brushes a hand over my shoulder, understanding completely. "I do. Those days are hard. You do your best, but sometimes it's not enough."

"Yep."

"But you keep going. You keep doing. It's all you can do."

"Yeah. You're right." I tell her why the shift hit me harder than most. I mention the thirty-six-year-old and how it brought so many unexpected fears to the surface.

She taps her sternum. "I can't make any guarantees, but this ticker is in solid shape. And I'm going to do my best to boss you around for a long, long time."

I manage a laugh. "You always were a third parent."

"And I probably always will be." She reaches for the door. "Come on in. Have some coffee and eggs. It'll make your day better."

It's early on Saturday morning, but the crew is already wide awake, crowded around the dining room table, playing a board game that looks nothing like the board games we played as kids—no chutes, ladders, or lands of candy.

Travis and Molly shout out their rowdy good mornings to me as Travis plays from the floor, entertaining Devon who is strapped into a bouncy chair.

"What game is that?" I ask Jodie.

"Imploding Kittens? Exploding Kittens? Kittens with Mittens?" She shrugs, whispering, "Trust me, I tried to get them to play Monopoly."

I do my best to ignore the name of the game, because I don't want to think about Perri. I stop at the table and peruse the cards. "I bet I can beat you guys, and I've never even played."

"No way! I'm an expert." Travis puffs out his chest, his dark hair sticking up in all kinds of Saturday-morning angles. I ruffle it as Jodie sweeps up the baby and sets her in a high chair.

"You can be on my team," Molly says, patting the chair next to her. "Devon's on Travis's team."

I drop a kiss to Devon's cheek, then snag a chair and join the kiddos for a rousing game.

Travis beats us, and I suspect it's my fault, since I was all talk. This game barely makes any sense.

But what does make sense is this. Being here. These kids. Their smiles. Chatting with my sister as she makes eggs. Feeding the baby a waffle. Soon enough, I've shucked off the cloak of doom from work, and I remember something I have in the side of my bike.

I head outside, grab the gift I tucked there the other day, and bring it in.

"Is it for me?" Molly asks, her big eyes sparkling with enthusiasm when she spies the wrapping paper and bow.

"Nope. It's for your little sister."

"She probably needs me to help open it though," Molly suggests.

"How thoughtful of you."

I hand the gift to Molly, and she assists—ahem,

does all the work—opening it for the baby, who's now perched on my sister's lap on the couch.

Devon grabs the pink hat and coos, laughing at it. She flaps it up and down like a pom-pom, then Jodie tugs it on Devon's head.

"That is the cutest hat I've ever seen. I almost wish it were cold out so she could wear it," Jodie says. "Where did you get it? I want to see if it comes in my size."

"Perri made it," I say on a yawn. "Sorry. Forgot to mention that. I think the coffee is having the opposite effect."

Jodie arches a brow. "Perri made it? For Devon?"

"She did."

Molly adjusts the hat on her sister. "Perri makes the best stuff. She's so fun and so nice, and I like her. Also, I like to draw animals, and I want to go work on a zebra."

Jodie lifts her chin. "Molly, why don't you and Travis go draw on the sidewalk for a few minutes?"

Uh-oh.

That means only one thing.

I'm getting a talking-to from the third parent.

Once they're outside, Jodie stares at me expectantly. "What's going on with you and Perri?"

Heaving a sigh, I drag a hand through my hair and sink down next to her. "Nothing."

"Is that what you want to happen?"

"No." I'm dead tired from denial. I'm exhausted from acting, with Hunter, with Jodie, and with Perri, like I'm not wildly in love with the woman I live with.

"So . . ." Jodie gives me that big-sister look. Wait, it's definitely the third-parent look.

"So what?"

"What are you going to do about the fact that you're in love with her?"

Yawning again, I shrug. "What is there to do?"

She pats my knee. "I could think of about ten things. Especially since I suspect she feels the same."

Hope dares to sit up and take notice. "You do?"

Jodie smiles wisely and pats the wooly pink fluff on Devon's head. "I sure do."

But then I remember Perri's words in the kitchen —our deal distracted her from work, and she doesn't have the time or the inclination to explore more. "Look, even if she feels one-tenth of what I do, she's not interested in relationships."

"Hmm." Jodie eyes the hat on the baby's head. "Yet she's interested in knitting hats."

"What are you saying, Jodie?" My eyes start to flutter closed. Night shifts are rough.

"I'm saying why don't you get some sleep?"

Seems about right. I'm ready to conk out on the same damn couch that sent me to Perri's house in the first place.

"Sure."

She nudges me. "I'm going to take the kids to the park. Travis has a nice bed. Go crash in his room."

She doesn't need to tell me twice.

In less than a minute, I'm drifting to dreamland.

When my eyes snap open, I'm not sure what time it is, or how long I've been asleep.

But Jodie's parked on the side of the bed. "Okay, it's late afternoon. And we're going to discuss ten things you can do. Are you ready?"

I rub my eyes. "Guess I better be."

36

PERRI

I twirl in the middle of the ice rink at Yerba Buena Gardens in the heart of the city.

Okay, it's not quite an accomplished twirl. But it does the job for an amateur, especially since the three of us did pretend we were Olympians back in the day, so we've mastered our *pretend* skating routine.

"Do a triple jump!" Arden calls out.

I peer around, making sure the skating police aren't looking, and I do a hop, hop, hop, landing each time without falling on my ass.

Score for me.

Laughing, I skate over to Arden and Vanessa, and we circle around the rink that's open year-round, chatting as we go. We catch up on little things and big things, talking about Arden's engagement to Gabe, about Vanessa's plans for the bowling alley, then a clever new storyline on Finley's TV show. We agree we need to head over to Hope Falls soon to see her.

When we're done with our hour, we skate off the ice, unlace, and return the rentals. "We'll be ready to try out for the national team any day now," I say as we laugh our way out of the rink and into the rare sunshine of a San Francisco summer afternoon.

Arden thrusts a fist in the air. "We're going to win the triplet team gold."

"Do they have triplet skating now?" Vanessa asks playfully.

"No, but they will when they see how awesome we are," I add, and we plop down on the nearest bench, where I sigh happily. We had sushi for lunch in Union Square, shopped for dresses for Vanessa on Fillmore Street, and wandered through Chinatown for trinkets before we landed here. I look around, drinking in the familiar sight. "I used to love coming here on weekends in high school with you guys. And then in college too."

Arden nods. "Slipping away to the city was always one of my favorite things to do."

"Same here," Vanessa adds.

I gaze up at the blue sky. "I needed this day."

Arden grabs her sunglasses and covers her eyes. "Yes, you did. Maybe we all did."

"Let's do it more often." But there's more I need to say. "And I promise, too, that I'll do a better job being open about things. That I won't keep everything inside till I'm reduced to a blubbering mess in Pilates."

"Pilates has that effect." Vanessa smiles. "But let's start with you telling us more about the man you fell in love with, so we can hear all the love secrets you were keeping from us."

My jaw drops. "Are you serious? Love secrets?"

Vanessa nudges an elbow into my side. "Fess up. You said earlier he gave you straightforward advice. Tell us more about what he's like."

My instincts rear up, telling me to shut my mouth, to stuff all my feelings deep inside the trunk in my head. But this time, I ignore them. I have to push past my hard shell. Taking a deep breath, I dive in and share my heart, telling them why I fell for Derek.

"He is straightforward. He was direct with me from the start. And he has this cocky edge that pairs perfectly with his huge heart. The way he is with his nieces and nephew is the sweetest thing I've ever seen."

The corner of Arden's lips lift. "Is that so?"

"Yeah. He's great with them. A total lovebug. But he also really looks out for them and makes sure they're behaving and treating each other well. And we had fun bowling."

"It sure looked like you did." A smile stretches across Vanessa's face.

I lower my voice, like this is the real love secret. "Also, he loves to snuggle."

Arden's eyes widen. "You landed a snuggler?"

"I didn't land him. But yes, he loves to snuggle, and he always wanted to spend the night together, and he usually made me breakfast the next day. Oh, that's another thing. He loves to cook for me."

Vanessa's smile enters another county. "He must really not want to be in a relationship with you."

I shoot her a curious look.

She continues, "Well, he cooks, he snuggles, he talks to you, he takes care of his family. He's also good in bed, you said?"

I grin wickedly. "He's magnificent between the sheets."

Arden's tone goes serious. "It really sounds like he has zero interest in you."

Vanessa nods in agreement. "Definitely. A man who'd cook, nuzzle, talk, and fuck like a god definitely has no intentions toward you."

A spark of possibility ignites in my bones. Have I been seeing this all wrong? Looking at the prospect of an *us* through the lens of our ground rules rather than seeing how our ground rules did a Cirque du Soleil–style flip the other way? Still, I'm cautious as I ask, "Are you girls messing with me?"

Arden pats my hair. "No way. He's for sure turned off by the possibility of being more than boinking buddies."

Vanessa adopts a terrible frown. "He absolutely can't fathom the thought of doing anything but banging you."

I roll my eyes, but inside, I consider their points.

Derek was awfully wonderful.

He absolutely behaved like a partner.

He completely acted like a boyfriend.

And you know what?

I do want that after all. I want all of him: roomies, benefits, friends, lovers, and more.

Sure, there's a hardened part of my heart—the part I need to lean on to be tough in my job—that wants to blot him out. But the bigger part—the soft, squishy part that loves her friends, that makes hats, that paints faces, that cuddles with Derek—wants to love him madly and deeply.

I want to love him with my whole heart, in all its various colors.

And I want him to love me back.

I don't know if he does, I don't know if he will, but I have to try.

While I lost out on the promotion, there will be other opportunities. The job didn't pan out, but that's okay. Things happen in their own time and their own way. But there might never be another man who fulfills me on every single level—heart, mind, and body—like Derek does.

That's the chance I can't let slip away.

I look at the time on my phone. "I wonder if we can make it to the kissing contest in time."

Vanessa and Arden turn into synchronized friends. "Yes, we can," they say together.

37

DEREK

I don't need ten things. All I need is one thing. A way to Perri. And Jodie gives it to me straight when I wake up that afternoon.

"The way I see it is this," she tells me as I swing my feet over the edge of the bed. "You love her. She clearly has feelings for you. The worst that'll happen if you tell her is that she'll kick you out."

"And then what do I do?"

"You come back here. You sleep on the couch again until you find another place."

I soak in her advice, letting it roll around, considering the implications. Really, when it comes down to it, that's not the worst. It's not what I want, but I'll be able to deal. It'll be no worse than where we're at now.

"It's that simple?" I say.

She nods. "It's that simple. Besides, you're only trying to protect your heart after it was broken. And guess what? Your heart doesn't have any protection.

There is no armor for it once you've let someone in. And she's in, Derek, isn't she?"

I scrub a hand over the back of my neck, noodling on her words. Perri isn't just *in*. She's everywhere—she's in my bones, she's in my heart, she's in my mind. "You're right."

"You have feelings for her. Deep and real and true feelings. You can either deny them or you can give them a chance to breathe and grow. See what happens."

Maybe I have been clutching tight to the idea of being uncommitted ever since my last commitment went belly-up, using my single status as a shield from getting hurt again. Because I'd be a liar to say the last time didn't smart.

But that's what happens when you open your heart. You take the chance that you could bleed, and bleed out. As I think back on the last few weeks with Perri, the nights we've shared, the times we've had, the reality is I'm already all in. I've opened my heart to her. The only thing left is to open my mouth and tell her the full truth.

Let the chips fall where they may.

"What do I do? Head home and say, 'Hey Officer Keating, guess what? I'm totally in love with you. Do you want me to move out of the garage and into your bedroom?'"

Jodie laughs. "Why don't you try something a little bigger?"

"Like what?"

She taps her temple, a sneaky smile stealing across

her lips. "If memory serves, the two of you were going to do some kind of kissing contest tonight. Seems like maybe that's where you ought to be sharing how you feel for this woman."

We put our heads together, and we figure out the way to do it. Then, in the middle of our plotting, Perri calls.

I tense as I answer, hoping to hear something good on the other end of the line.

38

PERRI

The blackboard. That's it. That's the answer.

My kitchen has been the nexus of our relationship, from the cooking to the late-night encounters to the blackboard.

"The thing is, I need to make sure he'll see the blackboard, and I'm not sure if he's home," I say to Vanessa as she drives. "Plus, if he's home, I'll have to slip in."

Arden waggles her phone. "Hello? It's called a phone. You use it to call him and tell him to check out the blackboard."

"Gee, thanks. I hadn't thought of calling him."

But truth be told, I hadn't. Derek and I have never been a phone couple. Or a texting one, for that matter. Our connection ignited when I pulled him over, and it sparked and sizzled in person, at the farmers market, in the waffle truck, and then in our home.

I don't think we've ever once dirty-texted each

other. Or flirty-texted each other. We haven't needed to. But now I desperately need to tell him something, so I dial his number.

He answers on the first ring. "Hey, you." His voice, and his almost term of endearment, hooks into me.

"There's something in the kitchen for you. Or rather, there's going to be shortly. Any chance you'll be home soon?"

"I can be home in fifteen."

I glance at the GPS in Vanessa's car. "Make it thirty."

"Thirty it is." He sounds hopeful.

I feel hopeful. "Bye, Derek."

Hanging up, I tap my foot against the floor of the car, willing Vanessa to go faster while, of course, obeying the speed limit.

Soon enough, we arrive at my house. I run to the back door and dart inside while Vanessa keeps watch in the driveway. I grab the chalkboard and leave a message.

I don't want to text him my invitation.

I don't want to discuss tonight on the phone.

I want to give him my truth and see if he'll receive it.

Grabbing some clothes, I fly out of the house, slide back into Vanessa's car, and head for her place. I get ready in a flurry, taking a quick shower, pulling on jeans and heels, sliding into a green top, and blow-drying my hair. A little makeup, mascara, and pink gloss complete the look. My heart hammers at rocket speed, and I take several breaths to calm myself.

But I'm ready. I'm doing this. I'm going to walk into the hotel ballroom and let that man know he's a thief.

He's stolen the biggest piece of my heart that anyone has ever had. And he can keep it.

39

DEREK

Not gonna lie.

I'm a kid at Christmas, riding home. I park my bike, ready to run inside and see what's under the tree.

I open the back door, flick on the lights, and listen for her. I don't expect to see her, based on her call, but you never know.

The house is still, so I vault into the kitchen, hunting for whatever she's left.

My heart sings when I spy the blackboard.

My smile is out of control. It somersaults and backflips, and I don't ever want to forget this moment. I snap a photo of what she wrote, and then I get ready, dressed in jeans, a Henley, and my boots. I hop on my bike and ride to the Windermere Inn.

The whole time I replay her note in my head.

What would you think if we revised those ground rules? We

could throw them out the window entirely and start over from where we left off the other night. If you like this idea, meet me at seven at the Windermere Inn.

I review my plan to tell her how I feel during the most passionate kiss category. When I reach the inn, I park and head inside, ten minutes before seven.

The sign for the fundraiser hangs from the ceiling of one of the hallways.

Kisses for dollars!

I walk to the check-in table, peering past it into the ballroom. A man and a woman on the dance floor are locked in a kiss, and I suspect they're in the marathon category. Other categories are listed on a sign on the wall—the movie kiss reenactment, the sweet kiss, the air kiss, and more. At the top of the sign, the name of the hotel is written in calligraphy.

That's when it hits me.

That's when I find a better plan. How to go all in. How to let Perri know in the fashion she deserves that my heart belongs to her.

I hoof it to the front desk, asking for Claire, the head of events and the mother of one marble-loving kid.

The skinny man at the counter tells me he'll find her, and a minute later, the brunette appears in slacks and a crisp blouse.

"Hey there, nose saver!"

"Good to see you, Claire."

"What can I do for you?"

"Well, the other day, you did say I could perhaps call on you for a favor, and I was hoping I could cash in on that."

"Hit me up."

"It's about the kissing contest." I gesture toward the ballroom, then I tell her my idea.

She furrows her brow, taking her time before she answers. "And it wouldn't really be an official category for raising money or anything?"

"No. I would just like it to be announced because I think she'd like it."

Claire smiles. "I bet she'll love it. Let me go talk to the event organizer and ask them to do it. Give me five."

I wait, checking the time until she returns a few minutes later, giving me a thumbs-up. "You're on in three minutes."

"And I can't thank you enough."

"Go get your girl," she says with a wink.

When I walk into the ballroom, I spot Perri in the far corner, chatting with Vanessa and Arden. It's one minute till seven. My lovely redhead fiddles with her shirtsleeves and flicks her hair off her shoulders. I want to tell her she's perfect in anything and everything and nothing.

And I will.

I stride across the room, passing the lip-locked couples and weaving past a pair of women who've entered in the reenactment category, doing Scarlett and Rhett as two ladies. *More power to them.*

As I pass Scarlett, Perri's eyes land on me. A hint of nerves seems to flicker across those green irises. But when I smile at her, locking eyes, the nerves disappear.

I reach her, wanting to yank her into my arms and kiss her senseless. But first, words. "I found your note."

"Seems you did." Her voice is nervous, but hopeful.

"It was perfect and beautiful, and my answer is—"

A voice cuts across the ballroom. It's the master of ceremonies, a Sandra Bullock look-alike holding a mic. "And now, we have a new category recently added to the lineup."

Perri stares curiously at the actress's doppelgänger. "I thought passionate kiss was next?"

I simply shrug, keeping my secret for another second or two.

The dark-haired woman speaks again. "And this category is the kind of kiss you give someone when you've fallen in love with them."

Perri snaps her gaze to me. The expression in her eyes is everything I never knew I wanted, and everything I have to have.

Wrapping a hand around her waist, I pull her close. "Want to enter?"

She whispers a shuddery *yes*, and that's all I need.

Taking her hand, I lead her to the middle of the

room. In front of everyone—her boss, our fellow Lucky Falls residents, her best friends, her parents, and so many people I'm getting to know—I kiss her like I've fallen in love with her. Because I have, and I want to keep falling in love with her every single day.

She kisses me back with a little bit of passion, a whole lot of tenderness, and all the love I could ever want.

When we break the kiss, I go first. "Just so you know, I'm in love with you."

Her smile can't be contained. "Funny thing. I'm in love with you too."

And when you've fallen in love, one kiss is never enough. I kiss her again, and as I do, the clapping begins, followed by hooting and hollering. Everyone cheers us on.

Briefly, I break the kiss, whispering to her, "Kitten, we're going to win the most passionate one too."

"We better." She grabs the back of my head and smacks a hot, wet kiss on my mouth, like we did in the waffle truck. She kisses me passionately, deeply, and with a consuming kind of fire. I kiss her like I'm going to be taking her home and fucking her and making love to her, because that's what I intend to do.

* * *

After that epic kissing fest, we grab a drink, holding hands and talking. There's so much to say, and words and truth spill out.

"I was so worried you didn't feel the same way, and that I was going to ruin everything," she confesses.

"I felt the same way."

"I was worried, too, I'd lose my edge at work."

I bring her closer. "I know you were concerned. What changed for you?"

She loops a hand around my back. "I didn't want to miss the chance at this kind of love."

My God, am I ever glad I decided to go for it with her tonight. "I'm not going to let you get away. Also, I'm here for you. I want to be the one you lean on. I want to be your support and your shoulder to cry on if you need one. I want to be the man you come home to, the one you know always has your back even if work is tough."

She sighs deeply, almost dreamily. "I'm taking you up on that. And I want to be that for you too."

"You will. You are. We can be that for each other." I kiss her forehead, savoring the sweet smell of her skin, the feel of her melting in my arms.

She hums against me. "What do we do next? Also, when can we get out of here and get naked?"

I laugh, loving her dirty desires. "How about as soon as winners are announced? And how's this? After we go home, after I get inside you, after I make you come five or six times and you're all nice and warm and snuggly in my arms, then we can talk about what's next. But I promise what's next will be even better."

She smiles up at me, splaying her fingers across my shirt. "You're such a snuggler."

I nuzzle her neck. "And you love it."

"I love it a lot. Kind of like how I love you."

* * *

We win two prizes, nabbing most passionate and the newly added one, since the event organizer said we nailed it so perfectly it simply had to be a real category. With my arm wrapped around my woman, we make our way toward the exit.

But the chief stops us before we reach the door.

"Keating, there's something I need to talk to you about."

40

PERRI

My nerves skyrocket as Jansen pulls me aside for a one-on-one chat. "Listen, I'm sorry to do this on a Saturday night."

My heart slams against my rib cage and all I can think is he's letting me go, that passing me over was the first step in saying sayonara.

I swallow, steeling myself.

If I lose my job, that will suck royally. But somehow, I'll manage. I have my friends, my family, and my man.

With my shoulders held high, I wait for him to say more.

He clears his throat, his voice a little gruff. "Listen, I know you didn't get the promotion, and I wanted to tell you why."

"Okay." I brace for impact. This is when the rug comes out from under me, but I'm ready.

His lips quirk up, and he grins.

The man actually grins.

"The reason you didn't get the promotion, and the reason I couldn't tell you right away, is I had some other paperwork to tend to." His smile widens like he can't rein it in.

What the hell? Does he like bearing bad news?

"I understand." I give nothing away, staying strong.

"I had paperwork to deal with because there's another opening. I think it's a good match for your fine skills." He takes a beat, and I'm not sure I'm hearing him correctly. Did he just say *fine skills*? "How would you like to be a detective?"

Chills spread over my flesh. The hairs on my arms stand on end. "Are you kidding me?"

He laughs, shaking his head. "I'm completely serious. We made an arrest today on the jewelry store case thanks to your intel. You impressed me with your commitment to solving it, and that's simply the tip of the iceberg. You've been a stellar officer. Every year you improve, and you excel. I wanted to give you the news the other day, but I had to iron out some final details to move you up the ranks. It's the perfect position for your experience, know-how, and smarts."

And I guess I don't have to wait for another promotion. An amazing one is coming my way. One I earned with time, attention, and dead-on focus.

Hell, I'm damn good at my job.

And I love my job. My smile takes over my face.

"You've demonstrated that you deserve it, and I hope that you'll accept," he adds.

"Thank you, sir. I accept."

I say goodbye to Arden and Vanessa before I leave, hugging them and thanking them for being the best friends a woman could ask for.

"You were my besties in grade school, high school, and now. We've been through everything, and I love you both."

They hug me back together. "Group hug," Arden says.

"Also, we decided you won the bet," Vanessa adds.

"I did?" I ask with a smile as we separate.

"Didn't you hear? Your most passionate kiss raised the most money."

I shake my hips. "I had a feeling we'd own that category."

* * *

We choose Derek's bed.

"The scene of the first crime," I remark.

"Then expect me to be guilty a helluva lot, officer." He smacks his forehead. "Excuse me. I meant *Detective Keating*."

I grin as I take off my top. "That's right. I want you to keep calling me 'detective.'"

"Can I call you 'detective' when I cuff you to my bedpost, put you on all fours, and fuck your sweet pussy with my tongue?"

I shiver at the tantalizing possibility. "My cuffs are downstairs."

"Then consider it an unbreakable promise for next time." He tugs me close, rubbing his hard-on against my hip through his jeans.

I groan, leaning my head back. "You need to get naked and inside me now."

"Then undress me, kitten. I'm all yours."

All mine.

Those words both turn me on and make me unimaginably happy at the same time. I strip off his clothes, he yanks off the rest of mine, and I pull him to me on the bed. Grabbing his chin, I bring his face closer. "I love you, Derek McBride. Will you fuck me like you love me?"

He nuzzles my neck with his trim beard. "Easiest thing you've ever asked me to do."

When he slides inside me, I feel *it*. Not just his cock, which I adore. But I feel the love between us. The intensity, the connection, the need.

He does fuck me. And that's what I want. He takes me like he loves me, like he needs me, and as I let go, I give in to love at last.

41

DEREK

A few weeks later

I raise the bar in another rep, and then one more while Shaw spots me. Once I finish, I wipe my hands and say, "You ready to grab a beer?"

"I'm always ready for a beer."

We head to the Barking Pug, trading stories about some of the crazy calls we've had in the past few weeks. Shaw's become a good friend in that time.

"You know what's cool?" I ask as we stop outside the bar.

"What's that?"

"That you never pulled one of those *don't date my sister* routines," I tell him as I push open the door.

"You never gave me a chance to, but I'm happy to do it now." He shakes a finger and adopts an old man tone. "Keep your paws off my little sister."

I laugh as we grab stools at the bar, but his laughter fades quickly as he clears his throat, turning more serious than I've ever heard him. "Speaking of, I need to ask your advice about something."

"Hit me."

"So listen, it's about Vanessa."

"Yeah?" I ask, remembering the chemistry between them at the bowling alley. "What about her?"

The bartender swings by, and we order. When he takes off, Shaw continues. "I don't know if you're aware of this . . ."

I'm pretty sure I'm aware of exactly what he's about to say.

"But I've kind of had it bad for her for a long time."

"I figured that out."

He looks at me. "Did you?"

"It's patently obvious. The two of you flirt with each other as if it's literally all you want to do."

"That seems a reasonable assessment." He heaves a sigh. "Trouble is, Perri's made it pretty clear she doesn't want anything to happen."

"She definitely has."

Shaw drums his fingers on the bar. "Do you think you could talk to her? Maybe try to smooth the path for me?"

I wince. "Ouch. I do value my life, you know that?"

"You're saying I have my work cut out for me if I'm ever going to go after Vanessa?"

I nod vigorously. "I'm happy to help you any way I can, but Perri is going to be one tough nut to crack."

Shaw rubs his hands together. "Then here's what I'm thinking."

While the bartender brings our beers, I listen as he tells me what he wants to do.

I raise a glass when he's done. "Good luck with that. I can't wait to hear how it goes."

EPILOGUE

Derek
A little later

Shaw juggles some chocolate chip cookies that Arden made.

"Look at that!" He tosses three in the air, spinning them in circles out here on the deck.

I clap a few times. "You're a master juggler, but I don't think anyone wants to eat those."

"That's cool. I do." After he lets the cookies fall into his palms, he stuffs them into his mouth, one after another.

"You're kind of a pig, Shaw," Vanessa calls out from the kitchen.

He winks at her, and I make a note to talk to Perri again later about these two. Pretty sure I have a good inkling as to what's up between them.

Perri's dad joins us on the deck, clapping me on the back as I help him at the grill on a Sunday afternoon.

"How's everything going at work, Derek?" he inquires.

Perri's dad is one sharp fellow. Smart, involved, and thoughtful. Her mom is pretty awesome too. I know because I go to her parents' house most Sundays for dinner. They've welcomed me into the family and treated me like her partner from the first time we met.

Sure, I'm still her roommate, but we share a room now. *Her* bedroom. Actually, we share the whole house, and all the bills. There is no more lease, no more month-to-month deal, and there are no more separate doors and hallways.

There is only one home, and it belongs to us.

"Work is good, sir. I landed a promotion and a raise, so I have zero complaints."

"Excellent. And how's everything with your sister?"

"Her husband is coming home in a few months, and Devon is walking, so Jodie has her hands even more full."

"But she has more hands to help her too," Perri chimes in from her spot lounging on a deck chair. "I happen to like the kids."

"Maybe you can give me a grandkid, then," her dad says, winking at her.

"Dad!"

He shrugs. "Just saying. Sooner rather than later

would be good." He leans in closer to me, whispering, "Maybe you could make her an honest woman, son."

I say nothing. I simply head inside and enjoy the meal with my woman, her family, and all our friends.

* * *

Later that evening, I unlock the front door and toss the keys on the entryway table. "I'm thirsty. Want some wine?"

She wiggles her eyebrows. "Wine is always a good idea."

"I'll pour some glasses. You get comfortable, kitten."

She sinks down on the couch, grabbing her knitting bag, pulling out the hat she's making for Jodie.

I head to the kitchen and open a bottle, but it's not wine. It's a bubbly beverage. Call me confident, call me cocky. Or just call me certain of this love.

I have a damn good feeling we'll be celebrating any minute.

I pour two glasses, set them down, and grab a piece of light-blue chalk. I write a message on the blackboard, then I call out, "Hey, can you help me with something in here?"

She chuckles. "What on earth do you need help with in the kitchen, Mr. Chef?"

"I need help pleasuring you on the kitchen counter. So get your sweet ass in here." Sex works wonders on the woman, and I suspect it'll indeed lure her.

Her boots click across the hardwood, and she turns into the doorway.

I drop to one knee and hold up the chalkboard.

I love you madly and always. Will you marry me?

Her eyes pop. She clasps her hand to her mouth. Tears well up. "Yes!" She nods vigorously, joins me on the floor, and kisses me passionately, even with the blackboard between us. "Yes, I'll marry you."

Happiness floods every damn cell in my body. "You haven't even seen the ring."

"I don't care about the ring."

"You better care. It's fucking beautiful. Just like you."

Letting the blackboard fall to the floor, I stand, her hand in mine, then I give her a glass of champagne. Hers contains a sparkling diamond on a silver band.

"God, it's gorgeous." Her green eyes twinkle with delight.

"I knew you'd like it."

She dips her fingers in, tweezer-like, to fetch it, and when it's in her hand, I take it and slide it on her finger. "Beautiful," I whisper.

She throws her arms around my neck. "By the way, have I mentioned how awesome this kitchen is?"

"This kitchen is everything."

I lift her up on the counter, and we enjoy another one of the great pleasures of this room.

ANOTHER EPILOGUE

Derek
A few years later

There are lies, damn lies, and then there's everything I've ever said about love at first sight.

It wasn't Perri who changed my mind. I didn't love her at first sight, and definitely not at first touch. It was after I got to know her and learned she was funny, sarcastic, flirty, and dirty, and had a heart I wanted to cherish the rest of my life.

But then, after we married, something changed in me.

Because something changed in her.

As soon as she told me she was pregnant, I was head over heels for the baby in her belly.

Now, as I hold my baby girl for the first time, I take it all back. This is love at first sight—a fierce, powerful love that I know will only grow stronger every day. This little angel is perfect, and I'm going to take care of her and her mother for the rest of our lives.

"I love you madly," I say to the tiny creature in the crook of my arm. She grabs my hand, and it's fitting—I'm already wrapped around her little finger.

I gaze at my amazing wife, who gave me this gift. Who gives me so many gifts. No one's ever made me feel this good. "And I love you so much too, kitten."

Perri smiles back at me, tired and beautiful. "Good, because you're stuck with me."

And that's exactly where I want to be.

THE END

Curious about Vanessa and Shaw's romance? Will these two give in to their desires? A romance like theirs is forbidden and oh-so-delicious! It's 99 cents if you preorder it! Experience their red-hot romance in NOBODY DOES IT BETTER! It's available on all retailers now!

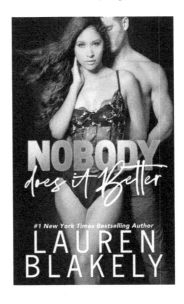

If you haven't devoured Gabe and Arden's sexy, swoony romance yet then you need to grab BEST LAID PLANS today! Available everywhere!

Another Epilogue

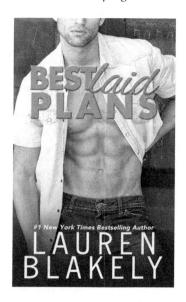

Experience this friends-to-lovers and lessons-in-seduction storyline that comes with a twist!

ALSO BY LAUREN BLAKELY

FULL PACKAGE, the #1 New York Times Bestselling romantic comedy!

BIG ROCK, the hit New York Times Bestselling standalone romantic comedy!

MISTER O, also a New York Times Bestselling standalone romantic comedy!

WELL HUNG, a New York Times Bestselling standalone romantic comedy!

JOY RIDE, a USA Today Bestselling standalone romantic comedy!

HARD WOOD, a USA Today Bestselling standalone romantic comedy!

THE SEXY ONE, a New York Times Bestselling bestselling standalone romance!

THE HOT ONE, a USA Today Bestselling bestselling standalone romance!

THE KNOCKED UP PLAN, a multi-week USA Today and Amazon Charts Bestselling bestselling standalone romance!

MOST VALUABLE PLAYBOY, a sexy multi-week USA Today Bestselling sports romance! And its companion sports romance, MOST LIKELY TO SCORE!

THE V CARD, a USA Today Bestselling sinfully sexy romantic comedy!

WANDERLUST, a USA Today Bestselling contemporary romance!

COME AS YOU ARE, a Wall Street Journal and multi-week USA Today Bestselling contemporary romance!

PART-TIME LOVER, a multi-week USA Today Bestselling contemporary romance!

UNBREAK MY HEART, an emotional second chance contemporary romance!

The Heartbreakers! The USA Today and WSJ Bestselling rock star series of standalone!

The New York Times and USA Today Bestselling Seductive Nights series including *Night After Night*, *After This Night*, and *One More Night*

And the two standalone romance novels in the Joy Delivered Duet, *Nights With Him* and Forbidden Nights, both New York Times and USA Today Bestsellers!

Sweet Sinful Nights, Sinful Desire, Sinful Longing and Sinful Love, the complete New York Times Bestselling high-heat romantic suspense series that spins off from Seductive Nights!

Playing With Her Heart, a USA Today bestseller, and a sexy Seductive Nights spin-off standalone! (Davis and Jill's romance)

21 Stolen Kisses, the USA Today Bestselling forbidden new adult romance!

Caught Up In Us, a New York Times and USA Today Bestseller! (Kat and Bryan's romance!)

Pretending He's Mine, a Barnes & Noble and iBooks Bestseller! (Reeve & Sutton's romance)

Trophy Husband, a New York Times and USA Today Bestseller! (Chris & McKenna's romance)

Far Too Tempting, the USA Today Bestselling standalone romance! (Matthew and Jane's romance)

Stars in Their Eyes, an iBooks bestseller! (William and Jess' romance)

My USA Today bestselling No Regrets series that includes

The Thrill of It (Meet Harley and Trey)

and its sequel

Every Second With You

My New York Times and USA Today Bestselling Fighting Fire series that includes

Burn For Me (Smith and Jamie's romance!)

Melt for Him (Megan and Becker's romance!)

and *Consumed by You* (Travis and Cara's romance!)

The Sapphire Affair series...

The Sapphire Affair

The Sapphire Heist

Out of Bounds

A New York Times Bestselling sexy sports romance

The Only One

A second chance love story!

Stud Finder

A sexy, flirty romance!

CONTACT

I love hearing from readers! You can find me on Twitter at LaurenBlakely3, Instagram at LaurenBlakelyBooks, Facebook at LaurenBlakelyBooks, or online at LaurenBlakely.com. You can also email me at laurenblakelybooks@gmail.com

Made in the USA
Middletown, DE
05 October 2023